THE LEGEND OF
SANGRE DE CRISTO COUNTY . . .

Setting his saddle gun aside, Longarm got out his six-gun and cautiously raised his head for a better look at the railroad shack.

A thin but still visible haze of gunsmoke lingered in the dark slit of the partly open doorway.

Longarm called out, "Give a holler if you'd like to surrender, Mister Fool Killer. For unless you offer some sign of less lethal intent I'll feel obliged to fire again, no offense."

There came no answer to that. So Longarm reloaded his six-gun, picked up his empty Winchester, and moved in for a look-see . . .

DON'T MISS THESE
ALL-ACTION WESTERN SERIES
FROM THE BERKLEY PUBLISHING GROUP

THE GUNSMITH by J. R. Roberts
Clint Adams was a legend among lawmen, outlaws, and
ladies. They called him . . . the Gunsmith.

LONGARM by Tabor Evans
The popular long-running series about U.S. Deputy
Marshal Long—his life, his loves, his fight for justice.

LONE STAR by Wesley Ellis
The blazing adventures of Jessica Starbuck and the martial
arts master, Ki. Over eight million copies in print.

SLOCUM by Jake Logan
Today's longest-running action western. John Slocum rides
a deadly trail of hot blood and cold steel.

TABOR EVANS

LONGARM

AND THE FOOL KILLER

JOVE BOOKS, NEW YORK

LONGARM AND THE FOOL KILLER

A Jove Book / published by arrangement with
the author

PRINTING HISTORY
Jove edition / November 1992

ISBN: 0-515-10980-0

Jove Books are published by The Berkley Publishing Group,
200 Madison Avenue, New York, New York 10016.
The name "JOVE" and the "J" logo
are trademarks belonging to Jove Publications, Inc.

PRINTED IN THE UNITED STATES OF AMERICA

10 9 8 7 6 5 4 3 2 1

LONGARM

AND THE FOOL-KILLER

Chapter 1

The winds were still gentle as they brushed and dried the high plains. But the last buffalo poppies had gone to seed, the cranes on the wing warned all who would listen of the winds to come, and Shavoka the Song Keeper didn't think his creaking bones wanted to carry the rest of him through another bitter powamu in this weary world where nothing worth singing about ever happened.

So one shining morning in the drying grass moon, as Tawa still shone warm enough, Shavoka strode forth in little more than a lot of strong puha paint to see if he could die a good death.

He had left the Spencer repeater Rope Thrower Carson had issued him many summers before with his other saltu things in that saltu house of his granddaughter, lest the ghosts of his own elders mock him as he came to join them in the humis hemis. He knew the crooked lance he'd won in battle with those who cut fingers would be more than enough to alarm the saltu who'd crowded in around here. But lest they mistake him for a mere vision seeker, he'd armed himself with a stout bow and many arrows, many.

Shavoka had been thinking a long time about the best place for a man with his songs to die. It was not far from where his kindly but terribly ignorant granddaughter lived with her saltu husband and disrespectful half-saltu children. But Shavoka had had a hard time finding the place again, after all the changes time and the saltu had made around here since that summer many stars had fallen.

The only things that had stayed the same were two smooth rocks, a little one and a big one, both rare this far out from the foothills of the shining mountains, where the creek that had once been more wooded twisted sharply to seek the wider river of the cranes. Choke cherries and elderberries no longer grew along the wide but shallow creek and the saltu had cut down the cottonwoods, all of them, to burn instead of buffalo chips.

Saltu were like that. The barbed wire someone had strung around the place he meant to die was stupid, too. Shavoka rolled through it as if it hadn't been there, despite his creaking bones. Then he was out near the center of the four fenced-in acres, near a square, wooden placard some saltu had mounted on two posts. Shavoka didn't know what the red-and-black marks on the white background said to other saltu. He was not a saltu, he was a real person and it had been just about here he'd won his first real fight as a boy of sixteen summers.

His good enemy had been a little older, unless he'd been painting lies on himself. In those shining times, before the saltu had found yellow iron in that very creek he'd just waded, those who had been first, the saltu called them Arapaho, had shared this part of the buffalo range with those who cut fingers, or Cheyenne. But neither had wanted the Ho or real people to live as fat and so there had been fighting, a lot of good fighting, in the shining times.

Singing, Shavoka drove the steel tip of his Cheyenne lance into the sod about where that other boy had died in the summer

2

many stars had fallen. Then he unwound a few yards of the long maroon satin sash he hadn't worn in many summers. Some of the paint he'd put on that morning had been made by the saltu as well. Few of the old ones who knew how to make strong colors from roots, bark, or duck shit were left, and a man had to look his best on the day he'd chosen to die.

Some saltu had planted trees along the far side of this place that he'd fought his first real fight. Shavoka had given up trying to understand such people. But now a saltu woman, a young one, in a dress that almost matched his sash, was moving along the walkway some saltu had made over there beneath the alien elms. It had to be a puha sign. Shavoka plucked the lance point from the sod and drove it through the trailing end of his sash, reaching for his bow as he called out loudly, "Here me, Saltumana who wears the same color as my last-stand sash! I am Shavoka the Song Keeper and from this stand I can move no more forever of my own free will!"

The white girl in the maroon dress and straw boater broke stride but kept going, less certainly, as she soberly regarded what seemed a very ancient lunatic they never should have let loose.

Shavoka wasn't sure he approved of her attitude. Shaking the bow at her, he shouted, "Hear me! I am really a dangerous person! You ought to tell the blue sleeves I am here in all my paint and puha to offer them a good fight!"

The girl stopped to call out soothingly, as one might humor a barking yard dog.

The old man insisted, "It was here, right here, I fought a boy bigger than me and won! It was here, right here, I lifted my very first scalp! But first I let him finish four verses of his death song. I didn't know what his words meant, either. But surely you can tell these words to you are serious?"

3

She apparently could. Gathering her skirts she turned to move off in another direction at a much faster pace than before.

Shavoka chuckled fondly and selected the right shaft from his elkskin waist-quiver to speed her on her way with a harmless but well-aimed bird arrow.

So Miss Prunella Clark of the Drovers Savings and Loan ran off through the downtown streets of Denver, screaming she'd just been shot in the derriere by wild Indians.

Chapter 2

It was fortunate for Shavoka, if not for all his dreams, that Deputy U.S. Marshal Custis Long of the Denver District Court was on his own way to work that morning, on time for a change, since it was payday and he was down to pocket-jingle. For Longarm, as he was often called by friend and foe alike, took his duties as a peace officer more seriously than some might take their back pay and hence, as the dulcet sounds of police whistles filled his ears, he swung that way instead of the easy way, without even breaking stride.

It was still a tight fit. The old Indian wailing like a banshee in the middle of a vacant lot made a swell target and the seven or eight copper badges who'd beat Longarm to the scene would have had him on the ground by now if they hadn't been commanded by Sergeant Nolan of the Denver P.D.

Nolan was still a sergeant because he was a tad smarter and way less murderous than some expected any lawman to be. He and Longarm went back together, some. So as Nolan spied the taller, leaner- and meaner-looking Longarm coming around the corner, Nolan shouted, "Don't gun him, Pard! Despite his paint he's a Treaty Ute who lives on my beat with his granddaughter and Silas Rutherford, the wheelwright. I sent one of my boys to fetch his kin. Anyone can see he's gone out of his mind but that short-bow he's been lobbing arrows with has a pitiful range."

As if to prove Nolan's point an arrow struck the paving about two-thirds of the way across Champa Street to skitter on to the sandstone curb at their feet.

Longarm nodded morosely and decided, "It ain't the bow. It's old age. I've seen a Ute put an arrow clean through a buff with one of them barrel-stave short-bows. But it takes a heap of muscle and . . . Hold on, I know that old cuss. I met him out to Camp Weld during the Shoshone Rising a spell back, dressed more sensible in his army blue."

Nolan nodded and said, "I told you he was on our side, until a few minutes ago, I mean. Bruised a pretty bank teller mighty sassy with one of them puny shots. What do you suppose got into him?"

Longarm sounded certain as he answered, "Old age. They don't look forward to it as much as we do."

Nolan said he wasn't looking forward to old age, either.

Longarm soberly replied, "It still scares them worse than we can try to understand. You see how he's staked his fool self to the sod with that trophy lance? That means he aims to go down fighting as many of us as would like to fight him."

Nolan snorted, "Hell, most any one of us could pick him off from a safe distance, right?"

Longarm nodded but explained, "He'd still feel that was a far better way to die than, say, in bed, coughing up crud."

A husky, sleekly handsome gent in a fancier suit than Longarm's just moved to join them and chuckled cheerful as a wolverine and opined it seemed only right that everyone should end this bullshit on a happy note.

When Longarm saw the stranger draw that lethal Walker Conversion from under his fancy frock coat, he just threw a

6

hard left hook and followed up with a wicked right cross as the stranger bounced back from the elm tree he'd just banged so hard with his head.

As the results crumpled at their feet and Longarm kicked the .45 out into the street, Nolan exclaimed, "Jesus, Mary, and Joseph, you just beat the shit out of our police commissioner!"

To which Longarm could only reply, "It was the least I could do. He was fixing to fire from the hip, the indifferent son of a bitch. Now make sure everyone holds his damn fire on this damn side of the damn street and let me see if I can head off an Indian war!"

. A couple of other copper badges seemed to think Nolan ought to have arrested Longarm for clobbering their boss. Their burly three-striper made some dreadful comments about their mothers before he ordered them to spread out and keep everyone out of Longarm's way.

By this time Longarm had armed himself with the galvanized lid of a nearby ashcan and headed across the street, his own .44-40 still in its cross-draw holster under the coattail of his tobbaco-brown tweeds. Shavoka waited until the tall, tanned saltu wearing a dark-brown telescoped Stetson lowered the improvised shield to roll through the barbed wire on that side. Shavoka saw it was going to be a good fight when the big but surprisingly quick saltu caught the arrow just in time with the edge of that unfair advantage.

"Woman heart!" the old man wailed in his own tongue, shaking a bony fist as he added, "No arrow can go through iron! None! You are twice my size. You have a gun that shoots six times. Why are you fighting so dirty?"

Longarm replied in English, "I don't speak that much Ho and few saltu savvy half as much. So if you've served as an army scout in your time you got to speak some American and I'd like to hear your revelations from the Puha Hemis, Uncle."

7

The old Indian's jaw dropped. Then he recovered, almost smiled, and said, "I know who you must be. You must be the one they call Saltu Ka Saltu, the one who arrested the crooked agent over at the Uinta Agency that time. I am called Shavoka. I am better known as a song keeper but I have fought some good fights in my time, too! Hear me, I scouted for Rope Thrower Carson when he cornered the Navajo in Canyon de Chelly and shot all their sheep. When some of my own people killed Agent Meeker and did bad things to his wife and daughter, I did not fight them, but I acted as a translator for the blue sleeves when Chief Ouray called for peace at Los Piños. I have not seen Chief Ouray since then. Is it true you people are keeping him back East in a cage?"

Longarm shook his head and explained, "Last I heard of old Ouray he was living in a fine log cabin over on the west slope of the divide. If it was up to some, we'd have him in a hospital lest you Ho blame us when his kidneys give out on him entire. But why don't we talk about your own troubles, Uncle?"

Shavoka sighed and said, "I have sung all the songs I know to grandchildren who no longer listen. Nothing is ever going to be worth singing about. But at least I can die on my feet like a Ho. Maybe someone will remember I was killed on a battleground of my choosing, by a fighter as famous as Saltu Ka Saltu!"

Longarm glanced down at the lance tip driven through the sash end on the sod between them as he softly observed, "I can see you staked yourself out here, Uncle. I would never ask a real man to unstake his fool self without a fight to the death. But ain't it a simple fact that friends and relations of a staked-out fighter get to free him from his vow? I mean it only stands to reason someone would *have* to if, say, the enemy ran away and there was nobody left to fight with, come suppertime."

8

Shavoka insisted, "I don't want you to be my friend. I want to die here, now, today. I don't want to go to all this trouble just to have people laugh at me."

Suiting actions to his words he took a vicious swipe at the taller white man with the end of his thick bow. But Longarm caught it with the rim of his ashcan lid, and said, soothing, "Easy, now, I don't want us busting such a fine old weapon, Uncle."

"Eater of rabbit shit!" the old man wailed in his own dialect as he plucked the Cheyenne lance from the sod and did his best to run Longarm through with the same.

He called Longarm worse things when he wound up on his painted bare ass in the grass. Longarm held the crooked lance as well as that ashcan lid, now. So the old Indian knew why so many of the saltu across the way were laughing, laughing, as if they'd just seen a young wife burn her man's corn pika on too hot a duma.

Then Saltu Ka Saltu turned to wave the lance at them and warn them to show more respect for real people. So when he turned back to say, "You ain't staked no more, no offense. Wouldn't it be best if we told everyone it was me, not you, who pulled this lance out because nobody here was brave enough to fight you?"

Before Shavoka could reply they both heard she-male weeping and wailing. So they turned as one to behold a fat young gal in a white gal's Mother Hubbard, with her Indian braids and headband, charging at them through the grass and weeds with her moon face wet as hell.

Shavoka sighed. "Now you've done it," he said as Longarm held out the butt of the lance to help him rise.

The proud old man's granddaughter shouted, "They told me you were drunk! They never said you'd gone crazy, crazy, painted like an infernal cigar-store dummy! And what are you doing with Willy's bow and arrows, you old fool?"

9

"Mind your manners, young lady!" snapped Longarm as the old man could only hang his head as if to cry. The granddaughter mistook his meaning, blanched, and pleaded, "Don't arrest him, kind sir. They told me about him scaring that white lady but I can handle him and I'm sure he meant no harm."

Longarm said, "I know what he meant, ma'am, and it's a mighty good thing him and me rode against the Shoshone that time. For as anyone can plainly see, he'd staked himself here for a last stand and nobody but a friend he was pledged not to kill could have got close enough to unstake him, so . . ."

The fat gal was assimilated, but not too assimilated to savvy his meaning. So she stared owl-eyed at her grandfather as she gasped, "Oh, no, you didn't! But you must have, now that some of the puha signs you painted on your own flesh come back to me! Oh, why would you want to leave us like that, Grandfather? Have we not fed you enough? Do you want more blankets on your bed? Haven't I told the children to stay out of your room when you are trying to remember the old songs of the shining times?"

Shavoka raised his head to stare thoughtfully at Longarm, who nodded slightly. The old Indian spoke American, so they could all understand as he said, gravely, "The shining times are gone. They will never come back. But maybe I have other songs to sing. I had forgotten the way I helped to stop a war at Los Piños. Saltu Ka Saltu has just reminded me how we rode against the Shoshone up in the South Pass Country that time and you can see what a close call I just gave the Denver Police, where once I killed a bigger boy of those who cut fingers."

The fat young matron understood Longarm's friendly gray eyes better now. She took the Cheyenne lance from him and softly said, "We'd better go home now, Grandfather."

So that should have been that. But as Longarm and the gal were helping the old man through the barbed-wire fence again

10

they were joined by Sergeant Nolan and a somewhat recovered but very irate police commissioner, who demanded, "What is the meaning of this? My sergeant, here, just explained the delicacy of the situation and since I agree it was wiser to take him alive I'll not press charges against you this time, Deputy Long. But why do you and your prisoner seem to be headed for that shantytown on the far side of Cherry Creek? Don't you intend to turn him over to the provost marshal out at Camp Weld?"

Longarm smiled thinly and said, "Not hardly. The army just got over one modest war with the Ute Nation and I doubt they'd enjoy another. Utes ain't as famous as your so-called Sioux and Apache because they rise less often, and fight way meaner."

He saw the politico meant to argue. So he told Shavoka's fat granddaughter to carry the skinny old man home and warm him up before he caught pneumonia in this tricky October air. When the police commissioner started to chase after them, Longarm slid his own ominous bulk between the damned fool and the fence, softly growling, "Don't make me kill you, mister."

The police commissioner gasped, "Sergeant! Did you hear that?"

To which Nolan could only reply, "Aw, I don't think he really means it, Commissioner. Tell him you don't mean it, Longarm."

But Longarm sounded as if he meant it when he flatly stated, "The last time the Utes rose they licked the U.S. Cavalry at Milk River no matter what you read in the papers at the time, and Utes rise quicker than most on points of honor. So given the choice of upsetting a Ute song keeper or the widow of a pissant politician, guess who I'd rather pick."

Chapter 3

Some born troublemakers come slicker than others. So Longarm got through the rest of payday without any trouble and it could even have been said he was lucky in both cards and love for the next forty-odd hours. He turned down an invite to a friendly little game of stud at the Black Cat after work and wasn't on the premises as a material witness when Four Eyes Peppard accused Doc McBride of cheating.

Better yet, a certain comely widow woman up on Capitol Hill decided she'd rather forgive Longarm for just a harmless fling than face a whole Saturday night with no better company than her own lonesome fingers. But Monday morn commenced on less comfortsome notes.

Longarm didn't learn he was in trouble until he got to work at the Denver Federal Building less than an hour late, despite a hard night in the saddle. He expected to get chewed out by his crusty superior, U.S. Marshal William Vail, because that was the way the two of them were accustomed to commencing every workweek. But he sensed he might be in for more than the usual remarks about clocks when young Henry, the priss who played the typewriter out front, warned him to get rid of his smoke before he went back to Vail's inner sanctum.

Young Henry was all right but they both knew Henry knew just how his bread got buttered. So Longarm didn't ask what he'd been accused of this time. He suspected he knew, in any case. So he just nodded and strode on back to Vail's oak-paneled office with the three-for-a-nickel cheroot still gripped in the teeth of a man with a clear conscience.

The older, shorter, and way-fatter Billy Vail only invited a caller to have a seat in the one decent chair facing his paper-cluttered desk when he was in a better mood. As Longarm studied the bushy-browed and jowly visage glaring up at him through its own haze of tobacco smoke he smiled back wearily, sat down without an invite, and removed his Stetson to use as an ashtray in case the old fart was really sore. He softly said, "I see you heard about my swatting that local official in hopes of heading off another Ute rising?"

Vail snorted like an old bull regarding a yearling trying to mount a manure pile and snapped, "I had to get that part out of a precinct captain I drink with at my club. There's no argument you were right to calm an important Treaty Ute down before any harm was done. What in blue blazes persuaded you to insult the U.S. Cavalry in front of witnesses, for no sensible reason I can come up with and I've been sitting here all morning, trying fit to bust!"

Longarm frowned thoughtfully, decided a few ashes would do as much for carpet mites at his hat, and put his hat back on as he replied, sincerely, "I never set out to insult anyone. Now that you remind me, I might have mentioned that ambush poor old Major Thornburgh rode into up to Milk River no more'n a year or so back."

"You said the Indians *won*!" Vail thundered, adding, "Is that any way for an employee of the United States Federal Government to carry on, you free-speaking fool?"

13

Longarm shrugged and said, "I thought freedom of speech was one of the things we had us a government to guarantee. What would you call close to sixty casualties with a field-grade officer numbered among the dead . . . a victory?"

Vail nodded curtly and replied, "The army does. They beat off a superior force of hostiles after killing at least a hundred of 'em, right?"

Longarm shook his head and insisted, "The Utes allow they lost less than forty, and they were the ones keeping count for their own side. With the army pinned down at Milk River for the better part of a week the Utes wiped out the White River Agency, killing another dozen-odd white men and raping all the women, young or not. I think they said Arvilla Meeker was sixty-eight. I can tell you the names of the Indians who led both attacks. They were Colorow, Canalah, and Quinkent. Nicaagat was involved as well. I'd almost forgot his brag on firing on Lieutenant Cherry in the middle of a parley. Would you like to tell me how many of 'em the victorious army got to hang after Chief Ouray got his boys to calm down?"

Vail grimaced and demanded, "Why did you think that sneaky son of a bitch told tales out of school about you to the sore losers at Camp Weld? Let's not split hairs whilst we study on how we get *them* boys to calm down."

Longarm sighed and said, "I wish you wouldn't send me way the hell out of town again so soon, Billy. I just got done promising a certain young lady I'd escort her to the opera, and not laugh at the tenor in tights this time."

Vail smiled despite himself and observed his wife had predicted a certain society gal would be unable to hold out and ought to be ashamed of herself. Then he said, "I'm not sending you out in the field to protect that widow woman's name. I'm doing it to save your job, you careless cuss."

He rummaged through the pile of papers in front of him as he continued, "Might be able to clobber two birds with one

14

rock if I can find the damned telegram. This white boy who raped an Arapaho laundress on a cavalry post was picked up by the Mexican Rurales as he was sloshing up the far bank of the Rio Grande and, seeing there was a reward posted on him, they settled for his boots and pocket change instead of the usual target practice. So even as we speak he languishes in the El Paso Jail, waiting for federal pick-up and transportation."

Longarm laughed incredulously and suggested, "Hang a wreath on your nose. Your brain has passed away entire! Picking up captured deserters is a detail M.P. noncoms fist-fight over! You say you want to soothe the savage military breast by stealing that twelve cents a mile and two-bits per diem from at least two regulars who could do with the restful train riding as well?"

Vail grumbled, "If you'd shut your fool mouth and pay heed to your elders you could likely spend more time at the opera. Did I say word-one about you picking up any infernal army deserters? To begin with, the fugitive is, or was, a civilian mule skinner who must not have known military terminology worth mention. For if he had he'd have known a pretty squaw described to him on an army post as a laundress was neither there to wash clothes or screw a mere enlisted man, let alone a horny civilian only hired to deliver a load of spuds!"

Longarm flicked his cheroot discreetly and said, "I know about Custer's Cheyenne household help. I'm missing something about this civilian who's about to discover everyone on a military post comes under military jurisdiction and that rape shall be punished by death or such other punishment as the court martial may decide. I still say picking him up in El Paso sounds like a sugar-plum detail for somebody in good with the provost sergeant."

Vail took the stogie out his growly mouth to growl better as he explained, "I didn't say I wanted you to mess with that murderous mule skinner. You're so right about the plans the army has for an asshole of *his* ilk."

Longarm blinked and muttered, "You must want me to fetch you some of them scented candles they sell in El Paso. You can buy a sack of cactus candy here in Denver for little more and who might our prisoner have murdered, that same Arapaho gal?"

Vail nodded and said, "That's how come there was such a bounty out on him. The officers she laundered for must have admired her skills. But I wish you'd quit thinking of the cuss as the plural prisoner of Justice and War. I keep telling you he's all their'n!"

Longarm nodded sagely and said, "You want me to bring back one of them mounted vaqueros the Mexicans weave so skillsome out of cornhusks, right?"

Vail said, "I want you to just hesh and pay attention. The Mexican Law, such as it is, turned the murder-rapist over to El Paso better than a week ago. The army naturally sent a two-man detail to pick him up. They naturally checked into a hotel near the depot and the jail to get a little shut-eye and an early start back in the morning with their prisoner."

Longarm said, "Naturally. I know the neighborhood and I just said it was a sugar-plum detail. I doubt they got all that much sleep, the gals in El Paso being sweet and cheap as cactus candy as well. But having pulled that detail in my army days, I'd say they were planning to take turns sleeping on the train, the next day. Prisoners headed back for a court martial don't seem as able to relax, but . . ."

"Both soldiers were gunned, from the front, side by side, as they paused for a nightcap in the tap room of their hotel. Both were packing issue Schofield .45s as well. And, no, neither was a recruit and neither had been drinking much when one gunslick took them out with exactly two shots."

Longarm whistled softly and asked, "In front of witnesses?"

To which Vail replied, "The barkeep and piano player couldn't get out of it. Everyone else who might have been there vacated the premises *poco tiempo*. The two Anglos who allowed they might have noticed a little trouble at one end of the bar agreed the killer seemed tall and dark, after which both get a mite hazy as to any descriptive details. The piano player says the killer might have been a Mex of the lighter persuasion. The barkeep, who just can't say whether he served the killer or not, allows he'd have recalled any damn greaser striding in, before any trouble might have begun."

Longarm nodded and said, "Most Mexicans who know El Paso feel more comfortable drinking a tad closer to the stock-yards. Is it important whether those M.P.s got into it with a Mex or not?"

Vail nodded and replied, "You speak at least as much Spanish as me and you've been down in them parts almost as often. So you must have heard whispers about El Matador de los Bobos by now."

Longarm chuckled and said, "Hell, you don't have to go down to Sangre de Cristo County to hear about the Fool Kill-er. The old folk back in West-by-God-Virginia tell the same warning tales about the ornery haunt. I reckon the legend of the Fool Killer goes all the way back to tales told around a fire in an ice-age cave. Country folk from many an old country have passed down the same ghost stories since Hector was a pup and if you've sworn out an arrest warrant on the the Fool Killer you're a fool he must have missed in his first few thousand years of wandering the back roads."

Vail insisted, "I never said those boys in blue were gunned by any haunt. The army surgeon from Fort Bliss was the one who said they'd been shot, each in the heart, with a .45. The point I've been trying to make is that we've had reports from all along the upper valley of the Rio Grande about a mysterious Matador de los Bobos or, have it your way, Fool

Killer. He's still a local want, albeit wanted in half a dozen counties, unless we can pin the two punctured federal uniforms on him. Meanwhile the army is naturally sending another M.P. detail, a bigger one, to bring back that horny mule skinner. So what I want you to do is hop an afternoon train down El Paso way ahead of them and see what you can do to assure 'em a safe return with their prisoner, whether you manage to nail the cuss as killed their comrades or not."

Longarm stuck the unlit tobacco stub back between his teeth, there being no damned ashtray on his side of the damned desk, and felt obliged to mention Vail's opposite number down El Paso way.

Vail sounded cheerful, considering, when he replied, "Oh, you won't have no trouble from the El Paso District Court or even the Texas Rangers, this time. Nobody but us seems anxious to go after undescribed gents who may or may not be living up to Mex gossip."

Longarm grumbled, "I can't say I blame 'em. We're talking better than six hundred miles by train to investigate a taproom shooting over who knows what betwixt two victims who can't tell me squat and a shadow nobody could identify for me in broad-ass daylight!"

Vail beamed and said, "I know. Maybe this time you'll stay out in the field until I've had time to save your job without having to sweat so much. Henry should have your travel orders typed up by now and the next southbound to El Paso leaves in less time than it would take a sissy to pack. So what are you waiting for, a farewell kiss?"

Chapter 4

Longarm didn't consider himself a sissy. But packing could be quite a chore when one's saddle and possibles were in one's hired digs on the unfashionable side of Cherry Creek and a fashionable widow woman in another part of town entire insisted on farewell kissing indeed. So Longarm wound up chasing the southbound at a dead run, with his saddle and possibles slung over a shoulder, as it was pulling out of the Union Depot.

He was mighty grateful for the help when a nicely dressed but sort of exotic young gal who'd been seated alone on the observation platform of the club car rose from her wicker chair to steady his McClellan saddle atop the rail as he barely managed to deposit it there.

For a heart pounding moment it looked as if she and his saddle might be headed for El Paso without him. Then he'd somehow managed a fistful of brass rail and she'd grabbed his wrist with a pair of surprisingly strong little hands. That gave him the edge a man needed to grab on with both hands as his booted feet got left behind. So he didn't really need her help as he hauled himself on up and over. But he still felt obliged

19

to thank her profusely and as long as he was at it, compliment her on her swell hands.

When he told her, rolling over the rail to join her, he suspected her of being a fine horsewoman, she confessed as friendly that her daddy grazed one of the bigger herds of New Mexico on one of the original Spanish grants.

He didn't say he'd already noticed she looked sort of Spanish. A heap of the old land grant clans were an intermarried mish-mash and whilst some, such as old Pete Maxwell over by the Pecos, were downright proud of their Mex relations, some could be proddy on the subject.

But when she said she was called Ramona Taylor he figured she was one of the relaxicated rancheras. For even Pete Maxwell shied at using his sprinkled name of Pedro.

As he introduced himself while depositing his saddle and such in a corner of the platform on the far side of the one other chair, he perforce caught a glimpse or more of what lay beyond the grimy glass of the club-car door. So he asked if she minded him sitting down out here as well. The smoke-filled interior offered standing room only and would have surely overflowed back out on the observation platform by now if the bar inside hadn't been serving the suds so skillsome. He knew why an unescorted lady had chosen not to belly up to the bar with the boys. But he still felt obliged to warn her she might have committed a tactical error in crawfishing all the way back here.

He said, "With the fall beef sales in progress and more than one trail herder paid off and headed home the easy way, we face a mighty wild time on this old train tonight. If my time-table means to keep its word, we won't be pulling into El Paso much this side of midnight and this club car figures to wind up way less sedate as the miles roll on and the boys drink more."

She sighed and said she'd already noticed, adding, "I thought I might refresh myself with a sarsaparilla soda as the train was

20

about to leave. Before I could even place my order at that bar in there a cowboy made a dreadful remark about my, ah, figure."

He'd already noticed she curved a mite junoesque, as short gals were inclined to do, under her tan poplin travel duster. But she'd just allowed she didn't cotton to having her curves the topic of conversation. So he smiled at the pretty oval face smiling back up at him from the shade of her polka-dotted sunbonnet as he offered to haul her forward to her proper seat while that might still be managed without violence.

She sighed and said, "Alas, it's even worse up forward in the crowded coaches. I wasn't able to book a private compartment this late in the day and you're so right about drovers headed home the easy way!"

He hauled the other wicker chair a tad closer and sat down as close as good manners permitted, to show anyone staggering out to join them that the lady was with him. He didn't ask her why she'd lit out for El Paso so impulsive. He figured she'd tell him if it was any beeswax of his own.

She seemed more interested in what he, his badge, and guns, had to deal with down El Paso way. Billy Vail hadn't sent him on any secret mission and they had a good twelve hours to kill, the Lord willing and the tracks remaining clear, but he wasn't as given to bragging as some. So he simply told her he was interested in those Sangre de Cristo tales of El Matador de los Bobos.

She didn't really startle him by laughing girlishly and telling him, "I must have been at least four or five years old the time I first hid under my bedcovers from El Matador de los Bobos, Deputy Long. He is no more than a *fabula de los duendes*. Forgive me. You would say a fairy tale, no?"

Longarm said, "No. *Folk* tale would be more like it where I come from. Us four year olds were warned about the Fool

Killer and he sounded more like a lunatic, or mayhaps an ogre, than any fairy."

She still stared wide-eyed as she insisted, "Be that as it may, you intend to arrest this legendary killer of foolish children who ask too many questions of strangers they meet in lonely places?"

Before Longarm could answer the door behind them slid open. So he half turned with an annoyed frown, saw it was a railroad ticket puncher he knew of old, and said, "Howdy, Max. We was just talking about surly strangers."

The conductor smiled back and decided, "I see you've heard the Kellog brothers have been stopping trains down around Raton Pass again and you've no idea how relieved the locomotive and express car crews will feel once I tell 'em you're on board."

Longarm could have told Max the Kellog brothers had bought the farm a few weeks back whilst resisting arrest in Nebraska. But not saying anything wasn't lying, and meanwhile they allowed him the same six cents and mile for moving his own baggage and self whether he paid anyone anything or not.

Assuming Longarm to be a more than welcome guest of his line, the conductor turned to punch Ramona Taylor's train ticket. She said the *dueña* she was actually traveling with had both their tickets up forward in perhaps the second or third coach car.

It sounded as reasonable to Longarm, alas, but he'd of course been hoping she might not be as traditional as her first name or flashing eyes might indicate. As the conductor left them alone again to work it out Longarm wondered how much time he had to work with before her dad-blasted chaperone came back to see what this pretty little thing might be up to.

She was asking more questions about that Fool Killer now. So he decided to save his money and let her damn *dueña* buy her that damned sarsaparilla once she came back to haul the flirty ranchera up forward some more.

He said, "My friends call me Custis and I ain't expecting to arrest no actual haunts, Miss Ramona. It's been my experience a real federal offense is more often committed by a real person."

She nodded soberly but insisted, "El Matador de los Bobos can hardly be a real person, ah, Custis. As I just said, I was first told about him haunting the Sangre de Cristos when I was no more than five, by a very old serving woman who said she'd been told about the monster when *she* was a child!"

Longarm smiled thinly and stared thoughtfully at the receding railroad ties as he replied, "The Fool Killer had been haunting the greener hills of West-by-God-Virginia since before that fuss with King George and his redcoats, too. Haunts don't worry about old age as much as the rest of us. Why don't I tell you how they describe the Fool Killer where I hail from and mayhaps you'll be able to tell me whether we're talking about the same haunt."

She said she was anxious to hear the Anglo version. He wasn't surprised. They'd barely left the truck farm belt around Denver and the surrounding scenery was already commencing to get rolling-grass dull.

It would have been rude to ask her permit to smoke without an offer to buy her that sarsaparilla. So he did without as he told her, "Nobody can say if the Fool Killer has a name, a home, or even a reason for the way he wanders the backroads or ridge trails by his lonesome, usually along about twilight. I know that makes no sense but they hardly ever tell of him meeting up with anyone by broad day and who'd be out in the woods alone more than a few hours after sundown?"

She nodded gravely and said, "El Matador de los Bobos sometimes rides. But he is most often met on foot, on some lonely trail, as you say, around sundown. Does your Fool

Killer change his appearance, as well?"

Longarm considered and decided, "Well, since so few get to live after meeting up with the Fool Killer, opinions as to what such a stranger might have looked like vary. To begin with, it's sort of tough to be sure you just met the Fool Killer out yonder if you're still *alive*."

She brightened and said, "We *do* seem to be speaking of the same dreadful creature. Is your Fool Killer not a very large but not a very ferocious-looking stranger who simply strides along the trail with downcast eyes and an unusual weapon, an antique musket, mace, broadsword, or something else as unusual in one hand?"

Longarm nodded and said, "That sure sounds like the same Fool Killer. The secret of survival, do you meet up with such a peculiar stranger in the hills of West-by-God-Virginia, is to howdy him as you would any other stranger you met up with in such tricky light and wait for him to do or say the next thing."

Ramona clapped her hands like a kid and chortled, "Let *me* say it! If you simply greet El Matador de los Bobos politely and let him pass, he will pass *you* with no more than a courteous nod. But if you ask him where he is going or why he is carrying such an odd weapon . . ."

"You'll have proven you're a fool," Longarm cut in with a wry smile, adding, "I don't see how they know his answer is that he's on his way to kill a fool or that his peculiar weapon is just the thing to kill a fool with, seeing nobody foolish enough to pester a mysterious stranger with such dumb questions at twilight takes another step alive. But, like I said, I ain't hunting for what I'd as soon call the unreal Fool Killer."

He indicated his McClellan in that corner of the platform and elaborated, "Haven't had time to go over all the reports I shoved in a saddlebag as I was leaving, but as I put it together, crude, scattered reports have come in from all up and down the valley of the Rio Grande about this morose individual who drifts in alone an hour either side of sundown, not saying much and not acting as if he might be on the prod until some poor someone *says* something to him."

She asked if he knew what anyone had said to the mystery man.

He shook his head and replied, "Can't even get a halfway good *description* of the cuss. Whatever the gents more interested in him might have said or asked, the results were certainly not at all what they must have expected. So far he's slapped leather on at least eight men, two of 'em military police with pistol ratings, and not a one had time to draw as he fired, once, fatal, smack through the breastbone at point-blank range."

She gulped and said, "Ooh, that *does* sound like El Matador de los Bobos!"

To which he could only reply, "They once sent me to look into one of them windigos or Indian spooks. When I caught him he wasn't even an Indian and I've caught more'n one dead man who wasn't so dead, after all, until I caught him."

The conductor came back again to awkwardly tell Ramona, "We got us a little problem with your ticket, ma'am. No offense, but there ain't that many ladies in the coach cars up ahead and not a one I asked seemed to be anyone's *dueña*."

Ramona looked sincerely concerned as she replied, "Heavens, I was sure she boarded this train with me back there in Denver! Are you sure she wasn't in one of those, ah . . . facilities as you passed through our car?"

Max said, "I sure am, ma'am. You've no notion how many try to beat me out of a fare by hiding in the, ah, facilities. So I make it my habit to watch, discreet, of course, as ladies and gents ah, respond to certain natural needs."

Then he hauled out his railroad watch and consulted it as he continued, "We'll be stopping in Castle Rock in half an hour to let folk on and off, ma'am. I hope you understand I'm

25

expecting to punch your ticket before we get to Castle Rock, or put you off there without no fuss as a favor to a lady."

Ramona didn't answer.

As Max moved back into the crowded club car Longarm sprang up to follow him. He returned in no time, but the pretty little gal was already dabbing at her face with a wilted kerchief. So Longarm waited until he was seated beside her before he held out the glass in his hand, saying, "They didn't have no sarsaparilla. But this here ginger beer ought to wet your whistle almost as good."

She didn't seem to hear him. But she must have known he was there when she sobbed, "Oh, Custis, whatever am I to do?"

He said, "Nothing. You don't have to get off at Castle Rock. I just got that squared away with old Max."

She gasped, "You didn't pay my fare! Whatever sort of a girl do you take me for, good sir?"

"A nice one, in some sort of fix," he answered simply, holding out the drink he'd bought more insistently as he continued, "They issue me six cents a mile and this line charges barely more than a *penny* a mile so let's forget about that part. I might or might not be able to be of more service if you'd like to tell me your whole tale, Miss Ramona."

So she did and it took her till well after they'd stopped and rolled on from Castle Rock. But despite its length, and importance to *her,* Longarm was having a tough time paying attention by the time she got to the part about leaving that two-timing brute with a drinking problem and winding up stranded in Denver when a slicker who used bear grease in hopes of hiding some gray hairs had told her the job he'd offered her in Leadville included some bedroom duties that sounded plain disgusting.

When she said even a woman who'd been happily married for at least a few years had to draw the line at crimes against her very nature, Longarm suppressed a yawn and said, "Right. So now we have to study on getting you back to . . . where? I was having a time locating a big Taylor spread on my mental map of New Mexico. Only Taylors I know with that much land graze their herds well east of the Texas line."

She sighed and said, "A sister who has always understood me may take me in, in Ciudad Juarez, if she can get her husband to ignore a little wicked gossip. I forgot to tell you that when I ran away with that two-faced Anglo he had this older wife who did not understand him and so we were never really married when he failed up in Leadville and . . ."

Longarm didn't want to hear any more about a willsome border teenager who'd persuaded her fool self that a man who'd cheat on one women could never cheat on *her*. He said, "I can stake you to a buggy ride across the border and at least some flowers, books, or candy so you don't show up on their doorstep empty-handed. In the meantime we'll be stopping again at Colorado Springs in a spell and there's no better way for us to move forward than via a dash along the platform there. Am I safe in assuming that carpetbag at your feet is all the luggage you managed to salvage from your Leadville adventure?"

She started to cry some more. He said, "Aw, cut that out. You already saw how good I can run with my saddle and possibles. If you can manage that one carpetbag we'll hop off at the Springs, lope on up to a coach just behind the dining car, and have us a swell jump on the stampede when they sound the supper chimes along about Trinidad, hear?"

She sipped some more of her ginger beer, regarding him sadly over the rim of the glass as she swallowed his words as well. At last she heaved a vast sigh and asked, "Just what are you expecting from me for all this largess, good sir? We both know I have nothing to give but my body and no matter

27

what you may think I am there are some things I simply can't do with even a man I love!"

He chuckled fondly and replied, "I ain't no 'good sir.' I'm only a naturally neighborly cuss and you sure have a vivid imagination if you think I was even planning to kiss you."

She blinked in disbelief, laughed despite herself, and coyly asked, "Not even one little peck on the cheek?"

He laughed back and explained, "Not hardly. All the compartments are booked and we'll be lucky to get seats together, up ahead. So why would I want to start something I can't finish?"

"You mean you *would* get fresh with me, if you thought we be able to go all the way?"

He said, "Sure. But since we can't, we may as well just ride on as friendly fellow travelers. You're pretty as any scenery we'll be passing this side of sundown and more fun to talk to than my own fool self. So can't we just be pals?"

She laughed like hell, recovered, and explained, "It's usually the girl who offers that suggestion, Custis."

He said, "I know. But don't it sound more novel when it comes from some old boy?"

Chapter 5

Mister George Pullman's newfangled dining cars were still as experimental as they were occasional on some lines. So the grub aboard the Denver & Rio Grande that afternoon needed just a mite more study.

But their coffee was good and strong. So Longarm washed down a thoroughly tanned steak and his literally half-baked spuds with a heap of it, knowing he'd be lucky to get a lick of sleep until the wee small hours.

From the way little Ramona stuffed her pretty face with such an ugly supper Longarm suspected she hadn't eaten anything for a spell. It made a man wonder what that bear-greased cuss had asked such a romantic-natured adventuress to do.

He didn't ask. He wasn't sure he wanted to know. Billy Vail had hardly sent him down El Paso way to get in bad with the border kin of an obviously impulsive young sass.

He washed down some petrified mince pie with another pint or so of black coffee. It wasn't long before he was wishing he'd had some more. They managed a coach seat together after supper and between the high altitude and sudden shock of not feeling hungry, Ramona's head was on his shoulder and she was either purring or snoring by the time they were rolling down the far side of Raton Pass in the tricky sort of gloaming light most train robbers admired.

Great minds seemed to spook at the same shadows. For when the conductor who'd mentioned the Kellog boys passed through after a flag stop he shot a mighty disapproving look at the pretty little thing who'd monopolized the shoulder of Longarm's gun hand with her sleepy head.

Longarm said, "I can doubtless wake her up as fast as anyone can stop a train, Max. But seeing the lady is so tuckered, would you mind reaching into the left saddlebag above us for the thin manila folder you ought to find sticking out of my other possibles?"

Max had to plant one high-button shoe between Longarm's boots to get at the saddle latigo-lashed to the baggage rack above the window. Once he'd unbuckled the saddlebag indicated it took him a spell longer to locate the folder by feel. As he handed it down he asked if it might be a dossier on the Kellog boys.

Longarm didn't have the heart to tell Max they were dead, the Sontags were likely out California way, or that Frank and Jesse had yet to stop a train this far west. So he simply said his home office would have all the current wants he was likely to trip over typed into his onion-skin orders and Max seemed satisfied.

But as the older man turned to move on down the aisle, Longarm said, "Hold on, Max. Whilst I got somebody to talk to, here, your worries about train robberies on this line, this fall, have had me just a tad puzzled. Who told you someone might be planning to mess up the timetable of the Denver and Rio Grande? No offense, but it's been my experience the target of choice in these parts is most often the Union Pacific, hauling bullion betwixt the Denver and San Francisco federal mints."

Max looked offended indeed as he replied, "I guess we haul us enough in our express car to show the U.P. a thing or two!

30

Swede Jarlsborg was the one who overheard some jailbirds jawing about a line off-guard and overdue some plucking."

Longarm started to ask a dumb question. But he was paid to keep track of names and so he nodded and decided, "Swede Jarlsborg is that sandy-haired railroad dick as foiled an attempt on the Salt Lake Line a couple of years ago, right?"

Max nodded and replied, "Blew Mormon Mike's brains out and put Paiute Pearson on the ground with a mighty sore shoulder that was barely starting to heal when they hung him."

Longarm nodded and agreed, "So we ain't talking about a railroad dick who don't know his trade. But I'm missing something, Max. Back up and explain to me how come an old pro like Jarlsborg only *overheard* a plot against the Denver and Rio Grande? Why didn't he throw down on the rascals and bring 'em in to elaborate in more detail?"

Max shrugged and said, "I wasn't there. But it's my understanding Swede was in one cell, doing a deal with another crook entire, and overheard the conversation in the next cell at an inconvenient time to show his hand. You'll have to ask *him* just who was saying what to whomsoever. All I know is that his agency transfered him to our line and we've all been alerted to keep a sharp eye as we traverse a heap of otherwise monotonous scenery."

Longarm asked if Swede Jarlsborg might be aboard, explaining how he and the lady dozing on his shoulder had moved up and down the train a heap along the platforms, during pauses along the way.

Max said he'd noticed and added, "Swede ain't riding with us on this particular run. Why did you think I was so happy to see you?"

Longarm chuckled and said, "I was happy to see you, too, albeit a mite surprised to see you on this line, Max. Since our Jarlsborg was riding another line when last we met, as well, how come?"

Max shrugged and said, "Speaking for myself, the Denver and Rio Grande offered a better deal for a married man working out of the mile high city with all its temptations for lonely wives. I told you, Jarlsborg was transferred by his detective agency. You'd have to ask him if he likes it better or not. I don't know beans about the galoot's personal life, and now I got to punch me some tickets or Lord knows *where* I'll be working."

They parted friendly. Longarm was sincerely sorry to see Max go. Mostly because now he had nobody to talk to and nothing to read but Henry's typing by tricky light. If he'd told Henry once he'd told him a hundred times to get a new ribbon for that gawd-damned machine. But the pasty-faced priss kept acting as if he had to pay for office supplies out of his own pocket-jingle and, come to study on it, the Denver and Rio Grande hadn't gone overboard on the lamp oil aboard this fool train.

But reading blurred type by the dim flickering light of swaying overhead oil lamps had staring out a grimy glass window at total darkness beat. For a spell, leastways. Henry didn't even hit the wrong keys often enough to make his field orders interesting and he hadn't included a word about train robberies or rumors of train robberies.

Aside from Billy Vail's orders to shadow and safeguard the army detail en route to pick up that same murder-rapist, Henry had dug out and transcribed the El Paso police reports on that mysterious shooting across from their jail as well as the charges and specifications against the old boy the army meant to hang, if ever their Trial Judge Advocate could prove his case as the general court martial it took to execute a cuss army style.

The horny teamster languishing in the El Paso Jail was not and never would be Longarm's prisoner. So he might not have boned up on that part as much as he had to if he'd had anything better to read.

It made dull reading indeed for a lawman who'd half dozed though many such open-and-shut cases in his time. The wretched sex maniac who'd only been paid to deliver them spuds behind the officer's mess had answered to the handle of Fernando Nash. After that it appeared he'd had the run of the post, or thought he had, during the time it had taken the kitchen police to unload his wagon.

Dying for a smoke but deciding he'd best not disturb the sweet little thing sleeping on his shoulder or the sour-faced old bat who kept glaring at the two of them from across the aisle, Longarm read on to where Nash had finally returned to his empty wagon and restless team, looking mighty jumpy, according to witnesses, and departed Camp Weld in a cloud of dust, not stopping at the gate, as if he knew the boys there had no orders to fire on civilians driving empty wagons in time of peace.

Turning over an onion skin, Longarm saw that, sure enough, that handsome and doubtless hard-rubbing Arapaho laundress had received a visitor, a Second Lieutenant Lewis, shortly after duty hours that same afternoon. Lewis had been let off the hook and Longarm agreed that made sense when it transpired, because within minutes of his yelling for the officer of the day, the naked lady he'd found had already gone into rigor mortis, meaning she'd been dead at least four hours or about the right amount of time to consider earlier callers.

The civilian teamster, who'd absented himself from his team the time it would have taken, worked better than anyone else on the post that day. Longarm wasn't surprised to read the dumb bastard had as naturally denied it. For who was likely to admit he'd ripped a gal's duds off and covered her bare brown hide with deep bloody bite marks after cutting her throat from ear to ear?

The provost marshal's investigative team had charged her throat had been cut before he got so passionate with her dead flesh and Longarm had to agree that made sense. The Arapaho play-pretty had been quartered in a shed described as a laundry, smack betwixt an officer's stable and their mess hall, and any gal getting both her nipples bitten off should have yelled loud enough to have had many a soldier blue hear her, had she been able to.

Longarm grimaced in distaste rather than in disbelief. Having ridden eight or ten years for the Justice Department, he no longer found it impossible to buy such transgressions as a display of mad passion to an already bloody corpse.

"I can see why they want to hang you, you disgusting piece of buzzard shit," Longarm muttered under his breath as he skipped a few paragraphs of pathetic denial to see what El Paso had to tell him about that more mysterious shooting since the original crime.

El Paso had made fewer notes than the army. Longarm knew hardly anyone who used as many words as the army to say anything. But it was mostly a shorter report because there seemed so little to report. There wasn't a thing here that Henry hadn't already told him. Army or more professional lawmen than El Paso seemed to have would have recorded more names. Longarm never neglected to name a possible witness just because he or she acted blind, stupid, or, in most cases, reluctant to be hauled into court, later.

At least, he saw, El Paso had placed the barkeep and pianoman on the premises at the time some person or persons unknown slapped leather on those military policemen for whatever reason.

Longarm made a mental note to question the prisoner they'd been sent to pick up as well. It was a longshot, but on the other hand the murder-rapist would have been spending this very night in the Camp Weld Guardhouse had not another murderous cuss blown away the detail sent to fetch him.

Thinking about that gave Longarm something to do as the train rumbled on through the darkness. There seemed no way to put the typed onion skins back in his saddlebag without waking a mighty sleepy lady and the Lord knew they'd made dull reading the first time through. So he finally managed to work the wadded-up sheets into a frock coat pocket and wedge the folder between his hip and the arm rest on his free side without an argument from a traveling companion that wasn't turning out so inspiring, either.

A million years went by. He spent a thousand or more undressing the ugly old gal across the aisle with his eyes. There was no way in hell he could justify the wedding band she wore on one bony finger. Trying to imagine the sort of cuss who'd marry up with such a frightful vision of sour frigidity helped him kill some time as well. He'd just established some depraved individuals were desperate enough to fuck a corpse and he supposed the old bag across the way had to be at least as attractive as a sheep, bareass and down on all fours.

He caught himself, smiled sheepishly, and killed more time by wondering why he wondered so often, so much, about more intimate moments of people he didn't want to get intimate with.

He told himself to think purer thoughts about, say, blood and slaughter. For sooner or later this fool train was certain to roll in to El Paso and after that he'd have to get off, late at night, with a pretty gal who had no better place to go and . . .

"Don't you even think about it," he muttered to himself as the steel tracks rumbled under them.

But of course he did and, try as he might, he had one hell of an erection by the time Max strolled through around midnight to tell him they'd be stopping at El Paso in a spell.

Chapter 6

El Paso was a border town and Spanish speaking folk got more done after dark than during the all-too-often scorching daylight hours of the horse latitudes. But Victorian notions of a lamplit Anglo world were tough to break. So most of the English speaking parts of El Paso went to sleep with the chickens and got to sweat like hogs during the sunrise-to-sunset working day anyone but a lazy greaser thought proper.

After having spent half a dozen of the past thirteen hours as a sleepy-headed gal's infernal pillow, Longarm was raring to go as soon as he'd gotten the pins and needles out of his gun arm and a couple of booted feet. As he lugged his saddle and led Ramona on out to the carriage ranks in front of the depot he observed a good half of the drivers looked Mex and that even the others were likely to know their way around Ciudad Juarez.

She said it was far too late to drop in on her sister unexpected.

He could have argued he'd met few Hispanic familes who'd refuse to take in a blood relation or, hell, the friend of a friend they might have met at a bull fight, on the civilized side of midnight. But he didn't, because he'd commenced to wonder whether Ramona *had* real kin in these parts. Her story tended to shimmer around vague edges as one tried to nail down names, addresses or other details. So he said, "Well, I ain't about to carry this loaded saddle and your carpetbag indefinite. I was planning on hiring a room over to the Eagle Hotel, which is near enough to walk if you won't let me treat you to a buggy ride across the border."

She said in that case she'd carry her own bag as far as their hotel.

Longarm let her. Neither he nor anyone from his office had told anyone he'd show up in El Paso at this hour and he'd almost missed that train as well. But it still felt better with his gun hand free as the heavy-enough McClellan rode his left shoulder above the cross draw grips of his .44-40. For neither of those dead army lawmen had expected trouble in this very neighborhood a few short nights ago.

He led her around the rear end of the carriage ranks and warned her the curb was high, which was a less crude but just as effective way to keep a lady from stepping ankle deep in horse shit. Most of the detraining crowd had naturally drifted the other way, whether they'd wanted to hire a carriage or not. Longarm made such tactical moves without really having to study on them after six or eight years at a sometimes dangerous job. As they crossed the fairly broad but dimly lit avenue Longarm felt obliged to tell the tagalong, "I've been known to hire adjoined rooms when traveling with a government witness, Miss Ramona. But you ain't no government witness, no offense, and my boss, Marshal Billy Vail, goes over my expense account with a fine tooth comb before he lets the accounting office say yes or no, if you follow my drift."

She didn't seem to. So he told her, less delicately, "When we get to that hotel I mean to hire a single, meaning one bed in a modest-sized room whether they allow guests after midnight

37

or not. So, as to my offer to see you safe to your sister's door, with us stopping for them flowers and such along the way . . ."

"I just told you I can't show up on their doorstep at this hour like the fallen woman my brother-in-law insists I am!" she insisted, adding, "Are you suggesting I can't be trusted if you let me get you alone in a hotel room, Custis?"

He smiled sheepishly and replied, "Nope. *I'm* the one as can't be trusted. You're a good-looking woman and I'm a healthy man and men are like that, no matter what their state of health, come to study on it."

She murmured, "Oh," in a small, thoughtful voice.

But when he repeated his offer to run her on over the border in style, she insisted she'd rather take her chances with him than her sister's sarcastic husband. So he muttered, "Well, Lord, nobody can say I didn't try."

The Eagle Hotel catered to working-class transients and looked it. So Ramona looked as if she was fixing to pee down a high button as she stood in the shade of a potted paper palm while Longarm bet the gray-faced desk clerk they couldn't hire him a single for less than a dollar a night.

The old timer was too wise in the ways of a man with a maid to look Ramona's way as he shook his head and said, "Buck and a half, seeing you're packing so much baggage, cowboy."

Longarm said he wasn't a cowboy but didn't argue with half fare for his pretty baggage, with no questions asked, as he signed in solo, albeit under his right name and office address.

When the room clerk noticed he murmured, "You might have told me sooner, but what's done is done and here's your key, deputy."

As Longarm took it the room clerk added, "Feels way safer this evening, knowing how many lawmen we got on the premises in case of another shoot-out next door."

Longarm had already noted the painted arrow indicating the way to the tap room for any thirsty guests. He asked what other lawmen they might be talking about. The room clerk replied, "Army lawmen, riding out of Camp Weld, Colorado, for the provost marshal. They ain't here yet. But they ought to be, soon. Their rail transporting officer reserved 'em a double, upstairs, by wire, this afternoon. Said they'd be arriving aboard the D and RG eleven forty-five and it's already a tad after midnight."

Longarm glanced at the Regulator Brand clock on one wall and saw it was running a tad fast. He didn't say so. He said, "If they're who I suspect they are we'll be meeting soon enough after one and all have unkinked their legs a mite."

As he herded Ramona up the stairwell she softly giggled and asked what the hurry might be. It would have been rude to tell a lady one was checking into a hotel with one who had other things in mind. So he simply explained he didn't want to introduce her to a couple of soldiers blue, adding, "Must have missed 'em aboard that train, what with all the wise money travelers ducking off or on such a rolling Black Hole of Calcutta. Like me, they've likely planned on resting up overnight whilst El Paso worries about that romantic-natured killer for all concerned."

Finding the right room in the dim lamp light up yonder was less trouble than unlocking a stubborn door with a now sort of heavy load balanced on the other shoulder.

Once they were inside, Longarm draped the McClellan over the foot of the brass bedstead and struck a match. As he was searching for something sensible to light it with Ramona moved to the one window and reached for the pull cord of the drawn down shade.

He said, "Don't," in a no-nonsense tone that gave her pause.

39

He saw it had and quickly added, "We can have this bed lamp lit or we can have that shade up. We can't have both because the window overlooks an avenue an easy rifle shot across, and I must have told you more than once, by now, they sent me to scout at least one old boy who smokes up us fools for no fool reason I've been able to come up with."

She crawfished away from that window as if she'd just noticed the sill was red hot, gasping, "Ooh, I'd forgotten all about El Matador de los Bobos!"

To which he grimly replied, "That's all right. I'm paid *not* to forget such matters. I'd best go back downstairs and tend to such chores before the whole blamed town goes to sleep on us. That'll give you time to get under the covers in such sleepwear as a lady might have in mind and we'll see how sleepy we both feel after I get back around, oh, say three or four with any luck at all."

She blinked in surprise and demanded, "Are you trying to ditch me, Custis?"

So there it was, right out in the open like a dog turd in the collection plate. So, seeing he couldn't gracefully ignore such a showdown question, Longarm soberly replied, "Had I wanted to I'd have done so by now. We've established you're a good kid in a jam and I've done about all I can, short of proposing marriage, to get you out of it."

She softly said she hadn't taken him for the marrying kind. So he told her she'd guessed right, adding, "I'm a tumbleweed type of gent with an uncertain future and no nice gal with a lick of sense would want to know me any more biblical than you already do."

She began to unbutton her travel duster as she quietly asked who he thought he was calling a good girl. When he soberly asked if she always traveled with so little on under her duster Ramona explained her one decent dress was in that carpetbag by the window and that she'd assumed the odds on anyone asking to peek under her full-length poplin duster had to beat the sure sweat and wrinkles of a long train ride.

He could only chuckle and agree it wouldn't have done him a lick of good to have guessed her secret aboard that train. When she coyly asked what he meant to do about it *now,* he was sorely tempted and said so, adding, "Hold the thought and feel free to start without me if I ain't back in two swishes of a tom cat's tail. It hurts to think of leaving you alone up here that long. But a man's got to do what they pay him to do and I know how much more it would hurt if I tried to stop in the middle."

She smiled knowingly as, tossing the entirely shucked duster on the bed, she moved in wearing nothing but her tight French corset trimmed in black lace and the shoes and socks she hadn't gotten to so far, allowing full inspection of her big bare lamplit breasts as well as the neatly inverted triangle of love-fuzz where her sweetly soft lower nakedness wedged down among her ample upper thighs. The legs, still encased in black mesh and high button shoes from frilly garters down, were as ample, but nicely turned.

Then she was kissing him, mighty friendly, and he got to feel a heap more than he could see with her seminude charms plastered to the front of him. He gave her almost as much tongue back in fair exchange and assumed from the way she was trying to unbutton his fly with her grinding groin that she could feel how much he liked her through the rough tweed of his fool pants.

But when she softly begged him to take them off he insisted he knew his own weak nature better, gently assuring her, "We'd both hate ourselves in the morning if we discovered I'd screwed up my mission while . . ."

"Screw me just once before you go back down those stairs!" she cut in, groping for the buckle of his gun rig as she tried to get them both closer to the bed.

41

He was way too big for even a plump little thing like her to wrestle and he told her so, with a mighty friendly goosing that made her squeal and let go of him just long enough to pop open the hall door, insisting, "I'll be back in no more than an hour, Lord willing and the creeks don't rise. Just got to make sure I got all the checkers on the board located in my head for the night before I get down to fun and games I'd like to give all my attention to."

She wasn't quite horny enough to follow him down the hall in no more than her corset, shoes, and socks. So she slammed the door hard instead, making the nearby wall fixtures flicker as he chuckled and made for the stairwell.

Partway down, he met up with a skinny kid in a bellhop's dull maroon livery, toting the baggage and leading the way for an all-too-familiar figure. She recognized him as well and disfavored a man she obviously detested with another withering look. Up until then he hadn't wondered who that ugly old gal across the aisle had been. He'd assumed from that wedding band, she had to be some poor bastard's wife or mother. Yet here she was, alone, in the sort of hotel few respectable women checked into even with an escort.

He didn't ask the sour-visaged old bat to explain herself to the law as he removed his hat and wedged himself into a corner of the dinky landing to let them past. She didn't offer, or even look at him as she grandly swept by in the wake of her baggage.

Longarm put his hat back on and moved on down to the lobby. He asked the clerk if the same barkeep and pianoman who'd sort of witnessed that shooting might be on duty next door at this hour.

The room clerk thought, then decided, "You just missed Long Tom Mahoney. Turned the bar over to his relief man about twenty minutes ago. Can't say who was on the piano that evening. It was my night off and piano players come and go restless as tramp printers and telegraph operators."

Longarm grimaced and asked if those troopers from Camp Weld had blown in yet. The hotel man replied, "Blown in and out. Just after you and your, ah, guest went on up. A Sergeant Plummer and I think he said his sidekick was a corporal called Finch. They put their gear up in their third floor room and came back down. Said something about hot tamales and that jail across the way."

Longarm started to ask whether they'd taken any of their gear, say leg irons, back outside at this hour. It made more sense to go see for himself. So that was the way he headed next.

He doubted even a toady bucking for more stripes would sign out a prisoner at this hour if he *hadn't* just checked into a hotel for the night. On the other hand, a heap of toadies had sure been bucking for stripes, dumb, most every time he'd had any dealing with any army. As he legged it through the after-midnight darkness he tried to come up with a northbound ride this side of sunrise. There was no saying when a late night or early morning way-freight might pass through. Such arcane matters didn't appear on timetables any railroad printed up for their passenger trade. But he was sure the last northbound night train was long gone.

At the jail house a sleepy eyed El Paso turnkey confirmed his suspicions about the murder-rapist they had in the back for most anyone who'd take him off their hands. The two army men had just dropped by to make sure the soon-to-be-late Fernando Nash had not escaped. They hadn't seen fit to wake him up for no good reason. So they'd assured El Paso they'd be back for the son of a bitch in no more than say forty-eight hours and gone off, they'd said, to see if the hot tamales of El Paso were as hot as advertised.

When the turnkey added he'd advised the boys they'd pay less for the same spicy servings in Ciudad Juarez, Longarm could only mutter some dreadful remarks about a heap of mothers. For he was under standing orders to stay the hell out of Old Mexico lest he cause more international incidents while, at the same time, Billy Vail had told him to keep an eye on those soldiers blue until he knew for certain nobody was trying to keep them from picking up and transporting that same prisoner.

Fishing out two smokes and handing one to the turnkey, Longarm decided, "Tear-assing through the red-light district of a border town in search of other gringo pains-in-the-Mexican-ass could be dumb in broad-ass daylight. At this hour it sounds more like begging for trouble. They'll have been invited inside or robbed in an alley by now in any case. You say Nash is asleep, out back?"

As the turnkey lit both their cheroots he opined the poor asshole was likely sleeping light to begin with and didn't deserve a break in any case.

Longarm took a thoughtful drag before he decided, "Can't think of anything I want to ask him that others ain't asked already. If he's got a confederate out to help him escape I doubt he'd want to tell me. I reckon I'd best just go on back to the Eagle and wait for the army to return from its Mexican campaign."

They shook on that and parted friendly. Longarm strode a mite faster as he considered how friendly he'd parted with old Ramona. But duty was, dammit, duty and so as long as he was headed in that general direction Longarm veered around to the street entrance of the hotel tap room.

It was sort of dead in there at this hour. Longarm suspected they wanted to close and would have, had not a half dozen beer drinkers been playing penny ante poker at one corner table. Nobody danced while playing poker. So the upright piano against the back wall stood silent with its keyboard cover padlocked until future notice.

Longarm didn't suspect at least some of these late night regulars had witnessed that shooting at the bar he was bellied up to at the moment. He was dead certain. But after that it got tougher to prove. So, knowing El Paso, the Texas Rangers and Army had gotten nowhere by a more direct approach, Longarm tried just ordering a needed draft and leaving his change on the mahogany as he waited for someone to ask *him* some questions.

It was the barkeep's place, of course. He knew the boys at the card table were also interested as the barkeep asked in a desperately casual tone if he was staying at the hotel.

Longarm said he was, introduced himself as a federal lawman, and sipped some suds in silence as everyone busted a gut trying not to ask if he'd been sent to look into that shooting.

The barkeep had to, after waiting in vain for Longarm to go on. He said he hadn't been there the night those poor army gents had been shot down like dogs, a tad closer to the door than where Longarm was standing at the moment.

One old bewhiskered cuss at the card table just had to explain, "The killer was standing right about where you are, now, Marshal."

A less experienced lawman might have asked if the old gent had witnessed the rest of it. Longarm smiled sheepishly and explained he was only a deputy marshal, adding, "I doubt the Fool Killer is ever likely to drink in this place again, seeing he committed cold-blooded murder by good light in front of trustworthy witnesses."

That naturally inspired demands he explain just who or what a fool killer might be. So Longarm repeated the old legend and two of the Texicans had heard it the Mex way, with El Matador de los Bobos acting so peculiar.

The old bewhiskered cuss, who hadn't volunteered word-one to a lawman up until then, couldn't keep from opining, "It wasn't any haunt, or even a greaser, as tangled with them army

45

boys. He was Anglo as the rest of us and dressed not unlike your ownself in a dark Stetson, store-bought suit, and. . . . Did he have a mustache or no, Wes?" he added, turning to the saturnine individual who'd been dealing before things got more interesting.

Wes, if that was his name, shrugged and replied, "I wasn't in here that evening. But I do seem to recall some mention of long sideburns and a mustache. Mustache heavy as that deputy's, albeit blacker."

The older man stared thoughtfully at Longarm and objected that Longarm hardly qualified as a blond or redhead. But Wes insisted, "There's dark and then there's darker. The stranger who threw down on them soldiers had an even more Apache complexion and his duds and hair were the same dull black as a coal bin in a cellar with the lamp not lit."

Longarm said he got the picture but wondered aloud how it was safe to assume the killer had been a white man.

Wes said, "He was dressed like a white man, built like a white man, and moved like a white man."

The old cuss grimaced and said, "Men of any ilk who move like that boy did make me nervous. I mean, as you were likely told already, that dark mysterious cuss never *fought* with them poor boys. He just gunned 'em in cold blood, bang bang, like you said!"

Longarm insisted, "Somebody must have said something to somebody, first."

The one called Wes hesitated, then offered, "I can't swear to nothing, not having seen anything, but they do say one of the army men asked the stranger something, a split second before he gunned the two of 'em and just walked off into the night as if nothing at all had happened, while the smoke was still clearing."

Longarm asked if Wes had heard what the soldier had asked. The dealer shook his head and replied, "Who listens to casual

46

words a dozen or more feet away?" Then he decided, "Hold on. I do recall . . . I mean I heard, the one who'd started up with the stranger raised his voice a shade to *repeat* a question the stranger must not have answered."

But that was it. Nobody there remembered "hearing about" more of the conversation than that. So Longarm decided to finish just that one schooner and get on back up to another dark stranger who seemed less surly by far.

But he never. For just as he was raising the rest of his suds to his lips there came a muffled fusillade of gunshots from somewhere up above and Longarm was already moving for the archway that could be followed into the hotel lobby as, behind him, someone marveled, "Sounded like pistol play, somewhere upstairs in the old Eagle!"

Longarm saw the same room clerk staring wide-eyed at the stairwell as he tore across the lobby, drawing his own .44-40 along the way. Some gal was screaming down the stairwell, now, so Longarm tore up it two steps at a time. But he was relieved when he got to his own floor to discover most of the ruckus seemed to be coming from the floor above.

There were still open doors and staring faces all along that second-story hallway, however, so he bellowed for the edification of everyone on the premises, "This is the law. So listen tight. I want everyone who ain't a law breaker or material witness to duck back inside and clear these damn decks for such action as needs acting on, hear?"

Then he followed the muzzle of his six-gun the rest of the way, calling out again as he reached the third floor landing, took a deep breath, and crabbed sideways into the uncertainly lit third floor hallway in a gunfighting crouch.

Nobody seemed anxious to gunfight him. The hall was still hazy with gunsmoke but he could make out one uniformed figure sprawled rag-doll-limp under a wall fixture with its head in the lap of a kneeling comrade. The screaming was coming out

47

of that ornery old gal from the train, albeit the young corporal trying to comfort a somewhat older three-striper looked as if he might be getting set for some screaming any minute. So Longarm told them both to simmer down and tell him what was going on up there.

The ugly-faced old gal, who wasn't built half bad and likely wasn't aware her kimono was hanging open like so, simmered down to a barely intelligible wail to the effect a murder most foul had just occurred smack outside her chamber door. So Longarm told her to get back inside her chamber and cover that least-mentionable part of a strange lady's anatomy, for now.

It worked. As she crawfished out of sight to slam her hall door hard enough to chip paint, Longarm dropped to one knee near the soldiers blue and aimed his gun more toward the stairwell as he reached for a limp wrist with his free hand. The corporal who'd gotten to his sergeant first half sobbed, "I think he's dead. Did I get the son of a bitch who gunned him?"

Longarm didn't answer until he'd made sure they were agreed on why the poor bastard didn't seem to have much to say. Then he let go of the limp wrist and said, "He's gone. Which way did you say the other one went?"

When the obviously rattled survivor launched a tangled tale of total confusion Longarm stopped him, introduced and explained his own self to give the kid time to put his brain back on the tracks, and quietly suggested, "Let's start calm, with you and and your sergeant here leaving the jailhouse across the way. For that turnkey at the jailhouse had you boys down Mexico way to get laid, tonight."

The somewhat younger M.P. raised his head for a look around as he whispered, "Take it easy, Deputy Long! The poor old sarge was a married man and I'm engaged to a Denver gal as pure as the driven snow. I know what that dirty minded Texican thought when the sarge asked, innocent, where we could get us some famous El Paso tamales. We

48

found a cleaner-minded old Mex selling genuine hot tamales from a pushcart just down the way. They weren't bad, but to tell the truth there's a Mex just like him selling tamales just as hot near the corner of Colfax and Broadway, back up in Denver."

Longarm nodded and said, "I know. He's sold me some on many a crisp Denver evening. Let's get the two of you back here to your hotel, seeing you're starting to talk calmer, now."

Corporal Finch said, "The sarge, here, was ahead of me as we came up them stairs. So he got a way better look at the jasper I remember best as a looming figure in a cloud of backlit gunsmoke."

"Easy, don't get ahead of yourself," Longarm warned.

So Finch took a deep breath, shuddered, and said, "They knew one another from someplace. Leastways, Sergeant Plummer thought they might. Neither said nothing as they passed one another near that wall fixture just up the hall. I wish I could say I'd paid more mind to another hotel guest in this dark a hallway. But I never. So the first I knew of any trouble was when the sarge snapped his fingers after we'd both passed the stranger, turned to take a few steps after him, and called out a name."

Longarm asked if Finch recalled the name. The corporal shook his head and said, "I've been trying like hell to no avail. Maybe it'll come back to me. It wasn't an unusual name. If it had been I'd have remembered it."

Longarm nodded understandingly and asked, "Keep going after the late Sergeant Plummer called out to his old pal, Smith or Jones."

Finch said, simply, "The bastard gunned him. Just like that. I naturally went for my own gun as poor Plummer was going down. Can't say whether I hit him or not. I know he never hit me and that's a pure mystery, too, as soon as you consider all

49

the rounds we both got off at close range before my gun, at least, was empty."

Longarm stared thoughtfully at the Schofield .45 on the rug by the corporal's right knee as he reached for the dead man's holster, saying, "You'd best hang on to this loaded weapon until you've had time to reload your own."

When Finch asked whether Longarm thought the killer might be coming back, the more experienced lawman soberly replied, "That's for him to decide and us to consider. I long ago gave up trying to outguess less-rational folk than myself and someone has sure been acting irrational around here of late!"

He rose, his own loaded pistol down to his side as he reached up to trim the wall fixture brighter. By now the gunsmoke was no more than a pungent smell. So feeding more oil-soaked wick to the flame than the management approved of improved the visibility one hell of a heap and that was when Longarm first noticed what Finch had done to the neater army blues he'd doubtless started out in.

Finch noticed, too, and to his credit left his dead sergeant's head where it was as only a little more blood and brains oozed out of Plummer's shattered skull. Longarm said, laconically, the part about Plummer going down without even trying made more sense, now.

Finch sighed and said something about bullets making way bigger holes going out than going in. Before he finished they both heard boot heels, a heap of boot heels, coming up the stairs. So Longarm hung on to his sidearm but got out his wallet to flash his badge and ID as, sure enough, someone called, "Here comes the State of Texas and I better not see no guns trained unfriendly as I takes charge of this here whatever, hear?"

Longarm sighed and put his gun away, figuring this was shaping up as a longer night, on his feet, than he and that sweet little Ramona had been planning on. So as the Texas

Ranger and two El Paso beat coppers joined them Longarm flashed his own badge and said, "Corporal Finch, here, can fill you in on all I know, so far. I'll be right back, as soon as I have a word with a likely anxious pal I come down with from Denver."

As he was moving toward the stairs Finch was already telling the other lawmen about what sounded a heap like the last unprovoked shooting, albeit this time with a survivor.

But nothing the survivor had said, so far, did Longarm a lick of good. Longarm tried to guess who *else* might possibly be helped by some murderous mystery man carrying on like the mythical Fool Killer. When that didn't work he settled for just plain *loco en la cabeza* until something more sensible came down the pike. Homicidal lunatics were way more common than master criminals, in real life. Unfortunately, they were the toughest kind of killer to catch. Not because they were so clever but precisely because they killed with such point-less viciousness that a halfway sensible cuss couldn't get the point.

He opened the door of the second floor room he'd hired earlier to find it dark and silent as your average tomb. He softly called out, "It's me at last and if you're asleep I can't say I blame you, honey. But didn't you hear all that gunplay right upstairs, just a few minutes ago?"

Nobody answered. That reminded him the door hadn't been locked when he'd turned the key in it, just now. So he'd kicked it shut with one heel and slid along the wall a ways, gun out, before he called out again and, when that didn't work, struck a match.

For less than a full second he thought Ramona was teasing dirty atop the rumpled bedding with her naked body posed so lewd. Then he moaned, "Aw, come on, Lord!" as the full horror of what he was staring down at sank in. After that there was nothing better for a man in his awful situation to do but

51

fire a shot into the wall paper to attract some damned attention, strike another match to light the bed lamp near Ramona's wide-eyed little head and open the hall door some more for the others clumping down the stairs in response to that single gunshot.

The Texas Ranger was first on the scene, full of questions until he spied Ramona's mangled naked body sprawled in a come-and-get it pose atop the blood-spattered bedding, with two pillows under her dead ass. The ranger gulped and quietly asked, "Who was she, Uncle Sam? Anyone can see what happened to her! Some son of a bitch bit her all over as he was raping her and then he cut her throat to shut her up, right?"

Longarm shook his head grimly and replied, "No gal would ever let a man screw her that rough without yelling her head off and nobody around here heard anything but gunshots in this hotel tonight. So add it up."

The ranger did and marveled, "Jesus H. Christ! What sorry sort of freak could treat even a pretty gal that passionate after she was lying dead with her poor throat cut?"

Longarm answered, simply, "The first one who comes to mind answers to the handle of Fernando Nash. He's accused of doing the same to another gal up Colorado way a short spell back."

One of the copper badges in the doorway blinked and objected, "Hold on. I know who Fernando Nash is. He's that poor sick son of a bitch we've been holding for the army just across the way."

The other El Paso lawman on the scene agreed, "We got him in a patent cell under lock and key, even as we speak. So how just how do you figure he managed to treat this other gal, here, so mean?"

To which Long arm could only reply, grimly lipped, "That's what I just said, dammit!"

Chapter 7

There was nothing like an after-midnight shooting to attract a crowd. So Longarm and those first lawmen on the scene soon had a mite more help than the situation really called for. So once he'd taken simple statements from Finch, that ugly old lady and others who refused to disagree with one another Longarm left it to the state and local lawmen to pick nits as they put every poor witness through the same ordeal.

Neither army man had brought along a change of Class A Blues and the late Sergeant Plummer's pants were no more fit to wear at the moment than his junior sidekick's, what with all the piss and worse a brain-shot cuss lets fly. But Longarm suggested and that Texas Ranger agreed Finch ought to soak his bloody pants in cold water and vinegar or, better yet, lemonade, before the bloodstains had time to set.

Finch allowed he'd heard as much from older soldiers but asked what he was supposed to wear in the damned old meantime. Longarm's intent had been he just sit tight in his room while the hotel help rinsed out and stove-dried his pants and, come to study on it, the shirt he'd had on under the fortunately open uniform blouse. Then the state of Texas offered to loan the kid a fresh civilian shirt and jeans. So Longarm didn't have to worry about that detail.

The morgue attendants summoned by El Paso P.D. allowed they'd be proud to put the dead lady on ice pending a coroner's hearing and some friends or relations coming forward to claim her remains. But they seemed undecided about dead military personnel.

The hotel clerk protested and Longarm agreed it seemed sort of uncivilized to just let the poor cuss lie there till somebody at the War Department opened the damned mail.

Longarm told the meat-wagon crew, "Corporal Finch is changing his duds right now but I'll put a night letter to Camp Weld on the wire when I bring my own Denver office up to date in a spell. From my own limited experience with armies I'd say the provost marshal the dead sergeant worked for will wire his opposite number at your nearby Fort Bliss and they'll send in a detail to take the cadaver off your hands in due time."

The El Paso corpse collectors wanted to know why Longarm couldn't offer them some faster results by wiring direct. It was the Texas Ranger who snorted in disgust and demanded, "Do as the man says and I can see none of you never rode in the war. There ain't nobody up at this hour but the officer of the day, sergeant of the guard, and such. When did you ever hear of an officer who couldn't get out of pulling O.D. having enough authority to wire another post in the wee small hours?"

So the morgue attendants said they'd haul both cadavers away, for the time being, and the room clerk told that bellhop to fetch a mop and pail of vinegar water from the kitchen.

Longarm didn't hang about that long. None of the meager notes he'd made so far added up to much. A hasty search of poor Ramona's carpetbag didn't even give him *her* name,

54

for certain. The reason she'd been killed seemed disgustingly obvious. But nobody staying or working at the Eagle recalled anyone fitting the fuzzy description Corporal Finch could offer and, even if the sex maniac who'd murdered Ramona on the second floor had been someone Sergeant Plummer had recognized, what had he been doing up on the *third* floor, when it was generally agreed he didn't belong anywhere in the damned hotel?

It only took Longarm a few minutes to stride back into the El Paso Jail with some even more pointed questions. The same turnkey was still on duty and full of questions of his own about the excitement across the way. So Longarm invited him to tag along and listen as he questioned the murder-rapist they were supposed to be holding for the army.

Despite the hour, Fernando Nash hadn't been sleeping back in his dreary patent cell of bars and boilerplate painted an ugly shade of landlord green. As he rose from his fold-down cot Longarm saw Nash was a scrawny little balding cuss with watery eyes about the shade and intelligence of two raw oysters. When that turnkey offered, Longarm said they could talk as well through the bars and that he hadn't come to do anything else to Nash, just yet.

As he told them both what had just taken place over in the Eagle he tried not to let his own feelings show. But some must have, because the turnkey softly said, "Hanging strikes me as a sissy way to deal with a shit who'd kill a gal and screw her dead body. But this corpse-fucker ain't been out of that there cell in the better part of a week!"

"I never!" Nash wailed, clinging to the bars between them as if his legs felt rubbery as he protested, "I never hurt Arapaho Annie up to Camp Weld, neither. I've admitted screwing her. Hell, everybody screwed Arapaho Annie if they had the price. But I ain't inclined to bite and, even if I was, what kind of shit would want a gal after she was dead?"

The turnkey said nobody was arguing about Nash being a shit.

Longarm said, "I have to allow I was a heap more certain until just now. So let's review what they have on you, Nash. Criminal investigation is more an art than a science, so far, but we have worked us out some scientific or at least logical rules. Unless a witness or more saw the dirty deed really taking place, we got to start with who could have done it. We divide that part into who had a possible motive, who had the possible means, and who can't prove he or she was somewheres else at the time."

Nash whined, "They told me all that shit when they arrested me. I told 'em and told 'em I had no motive. Arapaho Annie put out for a damned old silver dollar!"

The turnkey whistled thoughtfully. Longarm explained, "She was good-looking enough to ask that much from officers and, just for the sake of argument, let's say civilians making way more than the enlisted men where she, ah, served."

He dug out three cheroots as he turned back to the prisoner to demand, "How come you lit out, clean to Mexico, if you were so all fired innocent, old son?"

Nash heaved a defeated little sigh and replied, "I spooked. I drove out to the post innocent, like I keep saying, and figured on some innocent fun with old Arapaho Annie whilst the K.P. crew unloaded my wagon. I swear I'd dropped by her quarters before, as friendly as anything. The warm natured Indian gal had already told me never to pester her after they'd blown Retreat, but she didn't mind picking up an extra dollar now and again when her more fancy friends were on duty."

Longarm handed a cheroot though the bars and lit it for Nash as he told him to keep going. So Nash said, "I knocked on Annie's door and when that didn't work I tried the latch. It was unlocked. So I ducked inside and, soon as my eyes got used to the light she scared the shit outten me, grinning up at

56

me that way stark naked with her throat cut ear to ear and both nipples bit clean off!"

"That's when most men would have hollered for the corporal of the guard," Longarm dryly observed as he offered a light to the turnkey.

Nash nodded but said, "I told you I spooked. I don't know what I was thinking of as I tore back to my team and wagon. A Cheyenne uprising, like the one as wiped out everybody in Julesberg that time, mayhaps. I could see as soon as I'd drove off a few miles I stood to be asked some mighty serious questions so, well, I just kept going and if I hadn't been right about them suspecting me I reckon we'd be having this conversation somewheres else. But it wasn't fair to wire all them lies all over about me, damn it! For somebody else must have murdered Arapaho Annie, see?"

Longarm lit his own cheroot and blew a thoughtful smoke ring before he quietly demanded, "If not you, who? You told us a true tale, just now, of a modest-sized military post run strictly by the book from Reveille to Retreat. It's true there were mayhaps a dozen other civilians on the post that afternoon. Every one of 'em but yourself can be accounted for during the mighty short time the killer had to work with."

The turnkey asked how they knew exactly when that Indian gal had been so abused. Longarm dryly explained, "She had, ah, lunch with two junior officers, at group rates. This poor unfortunate was seen tearing out the gate no later than four, and you just heard him admit he last saw her in a dead and disgusting state."

"But I never laid finger-one on her!" Nash wailed, demanding in a more certain tone, "What about other officers, or enlisted men who didn't have a dollar to spare?"

Longarm shrugged and allowed, "A base pay of thirteen dollars a month could encourage desperate thrift and Lord knows horny army men have been caught at some mighty

57

unnatural acts. But after that the provost marshal was ahead of you. They *did* demand an accounting from each and every officer and enlisted man on the post that day and, before you bring it up, no, none of the Colorado Guardsmen who train part-time at Camp Weld were anywheres near the post at the time you, or, all right, somebody invisible, was treating that laundress so mean."

Nash repeated it hadn't been him. Longarm snorted impatiently and said, "Let's stick with a murder-rape I know for sure someone else had to commit across the way this very evening."

Nash demanded, "How the hell should I know anything about that? Didn't you hear old Tom, there, assure you I've been locked up in here for days?"

Longarm nodded soberly and said, "I ain't accusing you of gunning that M.P. just now, nor the two a few nights back. It seems a heap more likely someone's trying to help you beat that court martial. So I'd best tell you here and now that it ain't going to work."

The turnkey seemed as confounded by that last remark as Nash. So Longarm explained, "It's happened before. Friends or relations of some old boy arrested for an unusual offense act as offensive in hopes of persuading us we're holding the wrong offender, see?"

The turnkey nodded and allowed it had crossed his mind that a lady didn't have her throat slit and her tits bitten off all that often. But Longarm growled, "Consider the odds on such disgusting events taking place in Colorado when this cuss was up yonder and in Texas whilst he was here and I'm sure you'll agree the odds get downright awesome."

The turnkey nodded again but objected, "This one couldn't have hurt them folk across the way. You're saying someone just tried to prove Nash innocent by being guilty of the same bad habits?"

Longarm shrugged and said, "I just now said it happens. As the old song says, 'Farther Along We'll Know More About It.' Meanwhile, I hope you keep a list of each and every person who might call on anyone you're holding back here?"

The turnkey said they surely did, but added nobody but a dozen-odd local state or federal lawmen had expressed the least interest in the poor shit since his arrest.

Longarm said he'd still like a look at their records. So the turnkey warned the prisoner to make sure he snubbed that smoke out right when he was done with it and led Longarm back out front.

Longarm found no call to question the good faith of any of the other lawmen recorded as having dropped by ahead of him to ask a picked up want the usual questions. So he and the turnkey parted as friendly a second time and Longarm headed next for the Western Union, back near the railroad depot.

It was now pushing three A.M. and half the street lamps had run dry and flickered out, making for somber shadows along the deserted downtown streets. So Longarm wasn't surprised to find the elderly telegraph clerk asleep in his chair behind the counter when first he entered. But the old gent woke up without Longarm having to yell at him. So by the time Longarm had composed an update to Marshal Vail on a night letter blank the Western Union man had wiped most of the gum out of his eyes and seemed ready to go.

Longarm composed a more formal message to the provost marshal up at Camp Weld as the telegrapher was getting off the first one to his own superiors. Longarm tried to make both the late Sergeant Plummer and the confused young Corporal Finch look good as long as he was explaining why Finch couldn't get over to Western Union at the moment. Then he allowed both he and Finch were naturally ready and willing to carry out any instructions. It never hurt to pat a fool officer on the ass and it was likely Billy Vail would agree to most anything

59

from Camp Weld that made a lick of sense.

There were others he might have wired this early in the game if he hadn't long since learned not to confuse a possible game of tic-tac-toe with more masterful chess.

Folks had been killed more mean than masterful, so far, so he settled for asking the telegraph clerk if there might be a tobacco shop open in the neighborhood at this hour.

When the Western Union man suggested the newsstand over at the railroad depot Longarm agreed it was worth a try, explaining he'd been handing out two cheroots to every one he'd smoked of late.

It was just as well Longarm wasn't afraid of the dark and that the depot wasn't all that far off in the same. For by this time an overcast had swept in off the distant Gulf of Mexico and all of the street lamps left didn't shed half the light of the missing moon. So the railroad depot was no more than a big black blob across the way with a couple of bitty gleams here and there to indicate there could still be some lamps lit inside at this hour.

Longarm had crossed the avenue and was striding through the even darker shadows of the overhang around the corner from the carriage ranks when he saw, or at least sensed, another late night strider on the walk ahead of him, striding his way. So he cheerfully called a howdy, adding, "Might you know if the newsstand inside is still open?"

The dark blur never answered and it was just as well Longarm had lived through the first time he'd ignored his sixth sense as a teenaged scout on his first night patrol. For this son of a bitch slapping leather on him was way better than that poor enemy picket had been that night along the Tennessee.

After that he had to be stark-raving mad, of course. For he put his first round smack through the space Longarm's chest would have been if Longarm hadn't thrown himself blind as well as sideways into and over a damned shipping crate someone had left in just the right spot to set a man on his rump in the dark as he was trying to get off a round from the hip.

The surly shadow fired at Longarm's muzzle flash, of course, but of course Longarm had rolled the other way as he'd fired and so it was his turn to peg a shot at the blossom of flame that almost put a buzzing bee of hot lead in his right ear.

Then at least a half-dozen dogs were barking, doors and windows were popping up or open, and Longarm couldn't find anything closer to shoot at.

He knew for certain it was over when a depot door swung wide to spill light across the walk where that other cuss had been. Longarm still lay low, hunkered behind the bulk of that packing crate, till a portly old cuss in a rusty black suit and French-style kepi came into view, waving his own sawed-off ten gauge as he demanded the near total darkness all around tell him what in tarnation it was up to out here.

Longarm had been shot at by a ten gauge in his time as well. So he stayed put as he soothingly called out, "I'd be a U.S. Deputy as confounded as yourself, station master. I'll own up to half of the shots you all just heard, inside, if someone would be kind enough to tell me who I was shooting back at, and how come!"

A more distant voice called out, "Might that be Longarm making all that noise over yonder?"

Longarm called back a more cheerful admission, adding, "Since he don't seem to want to take advantage of all this yelling back and forth in better light, I'd say he's run off. Don't ask me where. I can't even say where he came from!"

As that same Texas ranger and a brace of familiar El Paso copper badges shoved into view Longarm broke cover to ask the station master and others hovering in the open doorway behind him if they'd gotten a good look at a man, woman, or haunt who'd just stepped out here on the walk.

He wasn't surprised to hear that nobody had noticed anyone leaving the waiting room a few moments ago. He stared thoughtfully down at the long rectangle of lamplight and muttered, "Sorry. Dumb question. But that makes his recent actions even dumber. If he wasn't coming out of the depot he was simply coming up the damn street from . . ."

"Nothing down that way but warehouses and our switch yards," the station master volunteered.

One of the beat coppers recalled a colored house of ill repute beyond the coal tipples. The ranger snorted in dismissal. Then he decided, "Where the cuss came from before he staked out here ain't as important as where he went, after. Do you reckon you might have winged him, Deputy?"

Longarm shrugged and replied, "Lord knows we both threw enough lead. But he missed me pretty good."

He began to reload as he added, "Reminds me of that famous gun fight in the Long Branch, up in Dodge. Some of the names as well as details vary with the telling but everyone's agreed these two drunk cowhands emptied their guns at one another, point blank, at card game range, with nary a soul in the entire saloon getting so much as a scratch. You got to aim at a cuss to hit him and I'd say near-total darkness works as good as Maryland Rye to throw a man's aim off."

He reholstered his reloaded .44-40 with a thoughtful frown as he asked the ranger, "What makes you say the cuss was waiting here with my stumbles in the dark in mind? I hadn't known I was headed for this depot, my ownself, five minutes before I asked a stranger in the night an innocent question and . . . Son of a bitch if that's not the way everyone's always said it's *supposed* to happen!"

The ranger nodded and said, more surely, "Hell, I thought you'd already figured you just met up with El Matador de los Bobos or, as some call him, the Fool Killer."

Chapter 8

Longarm finally caught close to five hours of sound sleep in a spare cell at the ranger station, after establishing for certain that his ranger pal had been standing out front of the Eagle with others, plenty of others, during all that gunplay in front of the depot a good three streets away.

The rangers had dryly assured him they'd considered all the local witnesses who could put him in the tap room of the Eagle while Sergeant Plummer was getting gunned up on the third floor and some had even raised the question of where he'd been during that first shoot-out in the ever-popular Eagle.

It had been Longarm who'd pointed out the alibi Corporal Finch had for that one, since Finch, too, could prove he'd been way up in Denver that time and, come to study on it, the other times the Fool Killer had struck hither and yon the whole length of central New Mexico.

The rangers hadn't worried about lawmen shot by haunts or even lunatics outside their jurisdiction but, yep, they'd established young Corporal Finch up on the third floor of the Eagle, waiting for his wet uniform to stove-dry, all the time Longarm had been swapping shots in the dark by the depot.

Longarm mulled over everything he knew for certain while eating a light breakfast of fried eggs over chili con carne. He ate alone, with a heap of black coffee, lest he confuse his own pieces of a pure puzzle with the opinions and wild guesses of others. After he'd failed to form a sensible pattern from the pieces of the puzzle he was sure of he left the beanery near the ranger station with the hope of scouting up some more pieces.

As he strode the downtown streets of El Paso he was sorry he'd lay slugabed this close to noon. For that overcast had surrendered without a drop of rain to a cobalt-blue sky filled with nothing but one big old glare-down Texas sun and neither side of any El Paso street could qualify as the shady side right now.

He found an arcade now and again and even when he was forced back out into the glare he found some comfort in the simple fact that it wasn't August.

He'd naturally checked with the telegraph office again before taking that flop at the ranger station around seven. He went back, anyhow, lest those first wires back from War and Justice inspire second thoughts.

They hadn't. The army still wanted Corporal Finch and his dead sergeant to report in to Fort Bliss and stay put until the provost marshal could put some commissioned investigators on the scene.

Billy Vail wanted Longarm to stick around and lend War as much of a hand as they requested. Nobody seemed to care as much about a murder-rapist already under lock and key, as long as he stayed that way until more important matters could be dealt with.

Longarm felt sure the rangers would have told him if Fernando Nash had escaped whilst he lay sleeping in their cell block. He was almost as sure Fort Bliss would have sent an ambulance wagon in for the living and dead of Camp Weld.

But he wasn't paid just to guess and so he ambled over to the El Paso Morgue to see for certain.

It was a mite cooler but not as sweet smelling in the basement of the morgue. The surprisingly cheerful attendent said most of what they were smelling was a Mexican or mayhaps Pueblo she-male who'd fetched up on a sandbar inside the El Paso city limits at least a hundred miles south of where she'd jumped, fallen, or been pushed into the Rio Grande. As they passed the locker she lay in, out of sight but hardly out of mind, the attendant complained to Longarm, "Had she had the courtesy to float on around just a few more bends we could have pawned her off on Mexico, but no, she had to split open and stop bobbing in the shallows where some quality folk were planning on a picnic under the crack willows!"

Longarm agreed a surprise such as that could mess up a picnic worse than red ants, but added he'd come to study on the disposal of those two murder victims from the Eagle.

The attendant reached for one of the zinc-lined oaken doors of their up-to-date storage facilities as he explained, "An eight man army detail from their Graves Registration outfit picked up that dead sergeant early this morning, Deputy Long. Couple of coroner's clerks came by later, to look that dead gal over and scribble a few notes. Somebody said she was a Mex, with kin down the other side of the river. If so, ain't nobody come forward and there are limits to our patience."

He opened the little square door and slid what was left of a once pretty gal on a movable slab of zinc-covered breadboard as he added, "Running out of ice as well, but, so far, this one ain't so bad."

He was speaking for himself. Longarm had been braced for bad but poor Ramona looked just awful with all that blood dried to a shade of rust and the edges of every wound gone dark and dry as split apple skin. He demanded, "Don't a lady rate an autopsy or at least a full coroner's hearing before you

65

release her remains in this town, Pard?"

The attendant said, flatly, "She wasn't no lady, she was a Mex, and anyone who'd like to take her off our hands is welcome to her."

Longarm's distaste must have shown. The attendant quickly added in a defensive tone, "There's no mystery about her death. Anyone can see her killer cut her throat from ear to ear and chawed her all over like a damned dog as well, right?"

Longarm said, "Wrong. Who done it is still a mystery and I've a few other questions I'd like to ask an expert who might give a shit. So let's start with a good undertaker with a strong stomach within easy walking distance."

The attendant chuckled and explained how undertakers flocked to the neighborhood of morgues the way bail bondsmen set up across the way from a jail. Then he suggested the Fischel Funeral Parlours as hungry enough to pick up a Mex but professional enough to embalm a pretty one right.

When Longarm found the place, around the corner and in back of a cactus hedge on a rundown residential street, like that morgue worker had said, he suspected he'd been sent on a snipe hunt.

Such things happened. But the nice-looking dishwater blonde who came to the side door wearing a faded print summer frock under an apron didn't act surprised when he told her who he was and what he was looking for. She said she was Alice Fischel and to come on back to her kitchen with her lest she ruin the tuna pie she had in her oven.

He could tell as soon as he entered her roomy, clean, but care-worn kitchen that she wasn't baking any fool fish. Mexicans and a few knowledgeable newcomers to those parts described the sweet red fruit of the prickle-pear as "tuna." Some ate them out of hand while others found them a seed-infested acquired taste. But most everyone enjoyed them seed-strained and baked in a juicy red pie.

He said so, taking off his hat as the heat-flushed and flour-dusted undertaking gal waved him to a seat at her deal table and rustled up some coffee and almond cakes for him. When she warned him she was alas baking the tuna pie for a sick neighbor down a ways he assured her he hadn't come to bum grub off her. He told her what he had come for and quickly assured her, "The murdered lady was white Mex, mayhaps not even Mex at all. But if you've a policy against such clientele, Miss Alice . . ."

She sighed and brushed a wisp of blond hair from her pale damp brow as she said, "Come now, you were surely told I don't do half enough business to put on such airs, even if I thought it was the Christian way to run such a business. You say you're a lawman and that this person was murdered?"

Longarm nodded and said, "You might say I'm helping out a pal as well, Miss Alice. My notion was for you to, well, sort of see she keeps, tidied up the way she'd more than likely wish to be remembered, until we can locate some next of kin or, failing that, find some churchyard as might take her in."

Alice Fischel bent over to peek into the range of her oven as she replied, "I know this sounds awkward, Deputy Long, but may I ask what sort of a price range you had in mind?"

He washed down some almond cake with her pretty good coffee as he considered, then decided, "May as well treat her first class. A pretty lady don't die every day and right now they got her stark stiff and messy, over to the morgue. She did have a dress over at the hotel. She said it was her best. It surely was her only and, to tell the truth, it seemed a mite ratty as well as flashy when I was going through her things in search of some home address."

His hostess said, "I can put her in a fashionable-looking and not-too-expensive white dress, made for the, ah, trade, of cotton double starched for the occasion."

He said that sounded all right and said, "I'm sorry to bring it up in a lady's kitchen whilst she's baking tuna pie, ma'am. But I told you she'd been murdered, sort of messy, and . . ."

"We use a special filler, called mortician's wax, and it comes in various shades to match the complexion of the dear departed to a tee."

He could have argued, having attended a few funerals of badly mangled friends and foes. Instead he said, "I'm sure you know your own trade, Miss Alice. That's where we get down to delicate matters. I just learned the county coroner seems satisfied the late Ramona Taylor was killed with a severe but simple slash across her throat. After that it looks as if some maniac bit her all over and, well . . . had his wicked way with her."

"We're talking about a woman who was murdered and raped," Alice Fischel said more simply, leaving her oven door ajar as she stood back up, glanced at her kitchen clock, and added, "I don't have any help here since I had to lay my part-time teamster off. I assume a cadaver over in the morgue is more important to you right now than this pie in my oven?"

Longarm smiled thinly and decided, "They got her in a sort of ice box and it'd be a shame to spoil that pie, Miss Alice."

She came over to sit across the table from him with a way less formal smile as she said, "You seem a very understanding man and they are much easier to work with once rigor mortis subsides. How long has she been dead, Deputy Long?"

Longarm said, "My friends call me Custis, Miss Alice. She was murdered a little over twelve hours ago and you're so right about her being sort of stiff right now. Her time of death ain't such a mystery but, whilst we're on the subject, how long would you give an average dead lady to turn stiff, like so, after someone cut her poor throat?"

Alice Fischel shrugged and explained, "There's no such thing as average. Depending on the person's weight and body temperature at the moment of death, then taking into consideration the temperature and humidity of the death scene . . ."

"Say an average sized gal in fair health inside a frame shed on the afternoon of an autumn day a mile above sea level," he cut in.

She shook her head and said, "Too many variables. If it's any help at all, rigor mortis can set in as early as four or as late as twelve hours after death, with both the high and low figures most unusual. Six to eight sounds less surprising."

Longarm nodded soberly and said, "Four to six hours works out right for the army personnel who last saw her alive or first saw her dead. It works out just awful for a teamster who swears he didn't kill the one and couldn't have killed the other."

He saw he was confusing her. So he quickly brought her up to date on both murder-rapes, assuming either had been any such thing. She seemed smart enough to follow him as he continued, "They might have autopsied that gal up at Camp Weld that thorough. I'll ask as soon as I get the chance. Meanwhile everyone down this way assumes Ramona Taylor was killed by some sort of sex maniac and I'll allow the same simple solution crossed my own fool mind until I met up with a fool killer who surely couldn't have been interested in my fair she-male flesh!"

The fair she-male seated across from him blinked, smiled, and then asked more soberly, "You want me to determine, in the course of embalming and laying out Miss Taylor, whether she was violated sexually as well?"

Longarm looked gallantly away lest she feel worse about the way she was blushing as he softly said, "I know this ain't no way for a gent to talk to no lady, Miss Alice. You say you don't have any help working here that I could be a tad more frank with?"

She sounded really upset as she turned back to flare, "I guess I can examine the innermost secrets of another woman as well as any dad-blasted old *man*!"

He saw she was doing her best not to blubber and so to help he reached across the table to place a gentle hand on her wrist and assure her, "It ain't you being less than professionable. It's me acting tongue-tied about, well, forensic fornication?"

That made her laugh, a shade louder than she might have if she hadn't felt so flustered. She didn't seem to mind his hand resting on her wrist like a friendly dove bird as she recovered enough to say, "Professional is the word I think you were searching for and professional it be shall, because you need the information and I certainly need the business. It's indelicate to talk about but no great chore to determine whether a woman has, ah, enjoyed normal carnal relations with a man just before death."

He had to ask, "What about abnormal, after death? I ain't no sex maniac, Miss Alice. We're talking about at least two gals submitting awfully *quiet* to some mighty rough lovemaking, if there was any such activity at all, I mean."

She glanced back at her oven as she told him rather primly that she knew exactly what he meant and that she'd rather just confirm or deny the killer's necrophilia *her* way, after a peek at the dead woman's privates.

He said that sounded fair but asked, "Seeing you brought up the scientific term for some mighty odd habits, would you be able to tell me, scientific, just how common such habits might be?"

She snatched her wrist free and rose to her feet with blue eyes blazing as she flared, "You bastard! I really needed the business and this was all a trick to get something on poor old Reb Durler, right?"

He got to his own feet, saying, "Wrong. Don't know who in blue blazes you're talking about and if he admired corpses in such, ah, biblical senses, I don't want to know about it."

"Get out," she decreed in a desperately proud tone, adding as she pointed the way, "Get out and tell your friends who ride for El Paso County that I really did fire the old sop for showing up drunk for a funeral too many times and I still say those children who said they'd been peeking through my cellar window when we had Miss Gomez half prepared were lying, lying, lying!"

Longarm said, "You'd best take that pie out and follow me over to view Miss Taylor now, Miss Alice. For I see we got us a serious misunderstanding, here. I ain't trying to get no goods on any hired hand who might have been accused of enjoying his job too much. If I knew for certain it wouldn't be my duty to arrest him. As I just now told you, I'm after a rascal said to commit necrophilia on his *victims,* not his *customers.*"

She turned away and covered her face with her apron, bawling so hard it seemed only natural for him to step around the table and take her in his arms to comfort her. There was more to comfort than her shapeless faded dress let on as she snuggled against him like a lost child to sob, "Oh, Custis, I get so tired of having to defend me and mine as if we were all some sort of fairy tale ogres who lurked under the bridge to the graveyard. Is it my fault my father took up this trade after the war because they'd taught it to him good, picking up after Hood's Texas Brigade?"

He patted her shuddering back reassuringly as he softly said a lot of old boys had needed such services after marching a spell with the ferocious John Bell Hood. When he allowed old John Bell had given the Union Graves Registration details plenty of training as well she sniffed and said, "Pooh, the Yanks had plenty of first-rate equipment. My daddy and his comrades had to make do with what they could forage and no matter what you may have heard about grave diggers and gold teeth, the Confederacy took good care of its own."

71

"Both sides tried," he assured her, adding to himself, "I ain't sure why soldiers treat even the enemy dead so much nicer but it seems to go with soldiering, like Aura Lee or Taps. Would you like me to show you that dead lady now?"

She must have. She took her tuna pie from the oven and set it on a windowsill to cool. Then she told Longarm she'd only be a minute and took more like five to change into a trimmer and more expensive but way gloomier outfit of black taffeta, along with a sort of porkpie hat of black felt with a black lace veil.

Longarm didn't have to offer twice to help with other chores. As she led him out back and across a well-tended kitchen garth, she explained she usually hired extra hands by the day whenever she got lucky. As Longarm led her one black Spanish mule from a stall and hitched it to her rubber-tired hearse with curtained side glass, Alice hauled out an ominously long basket of shellacked wickerwork and loaded it in the back by herself. He didn't ask why they preferred to pick up folk they hadn't worked on yet in such a glorified laundry hamper. Real laundry could be sort of soggy and stinky, too.

Once they were set, Longarm offered to drive and she didn't care, since they weren't on such a formal errand as some. Naturally it only took a few hoof clops to carry them back to the morgue and that was only because they'd be headed the other way with more of a load.

Alice knew the morgue crew out front and in back. Longarm could tell she was on fair terms with them when they made no fuss about releasing the cadaver to her despite the lack of a death certificate, so far, as soon as she and Longarm explained they didn't mean to bury anyone before all the formalities had been played out.

One of the morgue crew agreed with Longarm that lifting the stiff form of Ramona Taylor into that wicker basket and toting her on out to that hearse was no chore for a gussied

72

up lady. But on the way back to her place Alice Fischel said they'd best stop by another address to pick up the extra help she'd be needing with that much modest but literal dead weight.

Longarm stared soberly at the mule's ass ahead of them as he quietly said, "I'd be proud to help in the interests of economy, Miss Alice. I meant what I said about treating the lady in back to a proper send-off. But since she was neither a prisoner nor a government witness at the time of her death I get to pay her way out of my own pocket, see?"

The morosely dressed but friendly little thing must have. For she nodded and said she could go as low as twenty if he'd like to forget that funeral dress and settle for a plain pine box.

He knew she was being more than fair and said so, adding, "As a traveling man who deals in such matters now and again I've found the going price for such services a tad higher. High as sixty, in more than one cow town I've been stuck in, with a cadaver I had no further use for."

She said that sounded more like highway robbery than a funeral within the means of the average working class family. She surely would have told him more about the day wages of El Paso had not he cut in to assure her, "I want Miss Ramona planted in a lead-lined oak coffin, properly dressed, unless her fool friends and relations come forward in time to save me from such foolishness. Is it safe to assume that either way you'll take a personal check, drawn on an out-of-state bank?"

She nodded graciously and opined, "I don't think you're being foolish. I can see she meant something to you. She was very pretty, in life, I mean. I'll see what I can do about that as soon as she composes herself a mite."

Longarm grimaced and said, "We never got to mean all that much to one another. I ain't even sure who she was and might compose be the proper term for the way they go all squishy after a spell of acting so stiff?"

The undertaking gal shrugged and explained, "It's no more than a continuation of natural chemistry. Living flesh contains a good many fats and fluids that are liquid at body temperature and more like tallow once they cool a bit."

He nodded and said, "I knew that. I bank my occasional card winnings and other windfalls against such rainy days as this one and try to get by on my base pay from one month to the next. Sometimes I wind up reading a lot, and I still say rigor mortis gives way to more tender meat for the same reasons a side of venison slices better just before it starts to stink."

She sighed and said, "That's why the skills my father taught me are a true art, despite the distaste some of my neighbors may feel for me and my business. Whether you think I'm a ghoul or not, it gives me a great deal of enjoyment to hear friends and relations say one of my subjects looks as if he or she was simply asleep."

He said he'd never called her no ghoul. By this time they were pulling into her back driveway and some snot-nosed kids playing in her alley ran off, screaming, at the sight of the mule-drawn death wagon.

Well dressed or not, Alice had to carry the light end of Ramona's basket as she led the way down some cellar steps. Longarm didn't ask how come undertakers favored cooler cellars as their work places. This one was neatly kept with white-washed brick walls and a north-facing cellar window to shed more light than heat on the big zinc worktable in the middle of the cement floor. As they set Ramona's basket on some nearby sawhorses Longarm saw some big jars of what looked like cranberry juice lined up on a shelf above a zinc covered workbench. He knew that wasn't cranberry juice. Since this was far from his first visit to such an establishment he knew what most of the syphons, syringes, catheter tubes, and such on hooks above the workbench were for. He repressed an uncalled-for shudder when his desperately calm gaze swept over the big undertaker's trocar she'd obviously cleaned and polished, like a well-used gun, since she'd last had occasion to use it.

The trocar was as much a tool of the undertaking trade as the bone saw was of surgery, and Longarm tried to assure himself the trocar wasn't used half as gruesome. But he still wished someone would invent a less gruesome way to keep dead folk from bloating.

The tool of choice looked something like a hand pump and was, in a way. A long, curved hollow needle that could probe into the damndest places and suck out the damndest crud stuck out of the cannula, or pump cylinder, about as big around and half as long as a baseball bat. Longarm knew what had to be done to poor little Ramona with that trocar and other such gear. Having been through the war and some Indian risings since, he knew how much worse it could be to leave a dead body the hell alone. As he and the lady lifted the still stiff Ramona out of the basket to place on the work table, bloody, bare, and waxen with her lifeless eyes staring blankly up at the rafters and her pale lips spread in a mirthless grin, Longarm muttered, "I'm sure glad they posed her more dignified than she was found, before she got so much like a side of beef. What do we do now, Miss Alice?"

She smiled wanly and said, "*We* have done quite enough, for now. I want you to find something else to do, or at least wait upstairs as I change into my work smock and tend to a few basic chores down here. I don't worry about cosmetics, let alone dressing them, until they're more relaxed. But the sooner one tidies them up inside the better for all concerned, so . . ."

He said she seemed short handed and that he didn't mind watching a skilled craftsman at work. But she insisted, "I'm no such thing. I'm a skilled crafts*woman*, and this subject was a woman too and, well, I'm sure she'd have felt some things are

75

our own little feminine secrets, if you follow my meaning."

He did. He'd almost forgotten he'd asked her to look up the dead gal's pussy for evidence. So he said he had a few government chores to follow up on and asked when she wanted him back.

She said she and the dead gal could use the whole afternoon as long as there seemed no hurry. So he went back up, unhitched the mule, and put it away with some water, and ambled back to the main parts of El Paso.

There were no messages for him at the telegraph office. Neither the rangers nor the El Paso P.D. had even managed to figure out who Ramona had really been. Both killings had made the afternoon edition of *La Prensa,* published in Spanish and read on both sides of the nearby border. So Longarm figured any real kin of the dead gal ought to show up any time now.

Going back and forth over all the ground he'd covered the night before, jawing with a heap of the same people, killed time pretty good while he accomplished little else. Nobody he talked to could give him a better description of the gunslick who seemed to kill even sensible folk for no sensible reason, unless it had been the one thing they'd had in common, a tad more respect for the law.

A moody cuss on the run with a hard-on for any lawman he might meet only worked to a point. Like the legendary Fool Killer, he'd mostly thrown down on lawmen who'd spoken to him first. Longarm wasn't sure what other victims might have said or asked the mean son of a bitch. But he knew he'd only asked a blur in the dark if the damned newsstand inside was still open. He didn't find that so foolish, let alone threatening, and how in blue blazes had such a moody cuss recognized anyone as anything in that light?

"He knew your voice," Longarm decided half aloud as he spotted a tempting sign above the sun-baked walk ahead. He nodded and went on, as if to clarify his thoughts by voicing them, "Say he'd just calmed down after killing and raping Ramona a short distance away. Then say he heard you, of all gents, asking whether or not a stand that was open was open. Nobody could have attacked Ramona whilst she was alone without making certain she was alone, so, right, it works, and all this traipsing around sure give a body an appetite."

He entered the Mex beanery, had no trouble finding a seat at the counter at this hour, and ordered a serving of migas, a Tex-Mex specialty it was harder to find up Denver way. In other parts of the Spanish-speaking world, migas was literally crumbs. But along this part of the border they rustled up a filling repast of busted up tortillas, scrambled eggs, peppers, cheese, and Lord knows what all. It washed down swell with German-style lager, Mex pulque being an acquired taste.

That gave Longarm the energy to hire a livery pony and, using their stock saddle, ride the modest distance out to Fort Bliss for a talk with a junior officer at the provost marshal's office next to their stockade.

Calling it a fool's errand might have been putting it sort of strong. After comparing notes by army telegraph, Fort Bliss and Camp Weld had agreed to go halves on the investigation, with the Texas post shipping the late Sergeant Plummer north lest his kith and kin miss out on hearing that rifle salute and last bugle call, while Camp Weld got to keep Corporal Finch at least as long as a full-dress army investigation took.

Nobody seemed to want Fernando Nash at the moment. When Longarm asked whether they'd considered the consti-tutional rights of even a cuss like Nash to a fair and speedy trial they told him not to talk so foolish about cases he had no jurisdiction over.

Longarm could have argued, but that really might have been foolish. For nobody, including him, seemed to be getting any-where with yet another murder-rapist who, whether he was working with Nash or not, surely seemed out to weaken the government's case against the shiftless shit-for-brains.

Keeping all that in mind Longarm headed back for down-town El Paso. He was taking a short cut across the railroad yards aboard the unfamiliar but so-far obedient bay when somebody spanged a high-powered round off a steel rail, close, inspiring the livery nag to buck straight up and come down facing the other way, with Longarm shamelessly holding on to the horn at an insane angle with his left hand whilst groping in vain for a nonexistent saddle gun with the other.

"That'll teach me to leave my McClellan and Winchester in any damned old ranger station!" He decided as, that rifle spanging way closer this time, he just let go to land on one hip and roll down the safer side of a modest rail embankment to the dulcet sounds of ricochetting lead and galloping hooves.

By the time he'd fetched up in a dry ditch lined with sun-flowers and tumble weed he naturally had his own .44-40 out. He knew he'd never hit anyone at rifle range with any pistol, but at least he might feel better firing back. So he raised his already dusty hat on a handy sunflower stalk to see if he could get a line on where the bastard had been shooting from.

It didn't work. Having missed, and knowing he'd missed another man with a gun, the cowardly prick had lit out again. Longarm only waited until enough yard workers were standing over him to assure anyone of this before he got up with a weary shrug and just went on his way, feeling mighty foolish about that damned Fool Killer.

Chapter 9

That cellar door was shut when Longarm returned around sundown to Alice Fischel's establishment. Since he'd come back by way of that alley he hunkered down for a looksee as he passed the one north window of her unlit cellar workplace.

There was still enough light to make out the now rather saintly looking form of the adventurous Ramona Taylor, reposing atop that same table in a sort of bridal dress with her hands folded across her well-stuffed bodice and a way more serene expression on her once-again pretty face. He saw Alice had fixed the dead gal's hair in a ladylike fashion after washing her good and doing something magical about her waxen pallor and gashed open throat.

Knowing they used theatrical powder and paint as well as that ruby mixture of poisonous preservatives, he still had to hand it to old Alice and would have told her so, right off, as he caught up with her in her unlit kitchen, had not the poor gal had her own head down on her table, bawling fit to bust.

She glanced up to see who it was in her doorway as he made some polite noises there. Then she put her head back down and blubbered something about only wanting to help.

He stepped inside and shut the door after him, lest her neighbors accuse him of scaring her as he softly assured her, "You done a grand job, Miss Alice. I just now looked in on Miss Ramona and I vow she does look as if she just fell asleep, as unoriginal as that may sound to you."

Alice glanced up, as if puzzled, then shrugged and said, "Oh, her. That's my job and, dammit, I'm good at it. If it's of any use to your job, she'd bled to death by the time those last bites were inflicted upon her and, yes, she had enjoyed sex with some man shorty before or after she died."

He blinked in bemusement and replied, "I doubt she could have enjoyed it, either way. We'd already figured she met up with a real monster and I'd have been more surprised to find she'd died more chaste. I'm sorry all this upset you so, Miss Alice."

She really looked puzzled as she sat up straighter to tell him, "Good heavens, I don't let my family trade upset me that much! I really shouldn't have given way to other feelings that way, just now. You'd think the neighborhood ghoul would be used to being an object of distaste and superstitious fear by now, but honestly, I never thought Rosa Moreno would respond that unkindly to my simple gesture to a sick neighbor!"

By this time Longarm had already noticed that tuna pie, now as cool as it needed to get, on that same windowsill. So he nodded and softly said, "Superstitious fear makes heaps of otherwise good folk act silly, Miss Alice. Just ask the good folk of Salem, back East."

She sobbed, "For God's sake, I wash with naptha soap between times and I hadn't had any business for weeks when I started that pie for them this morning. When I sent a neighborhood child to tell them it was ready they sent him back with a very rude message and I ask you, what in heaven's name might I have occasion to touch that their family doctor doesn't handle more often?"

Longarm soothed, "Folk only say they believe in heaven as they whistle by the graveyard late at night, Miss Alice. I'd be proud to eat that tuna pie for you and kiss your pretty wrist as a reward for second helpings. But I got to admit it gave me just a tiny turn, downstairs, to consider what you were fixing to do to a lady I knew with that big brass trocar."

She started to protest. He stopped her, saying, "Hold on. You asked for reasons. I'm trying to give some to you. Unlike your witless neighbors, I knew what was upsetting me when I pictured you at work on that other gal's innards with your trocar."

She pleaded, "Custis, it has to be done, unless one follows the Hebrew custom of instant burial. As I told you, before, chemistry dosen't quit when our other life processes do. The digestive fluids keep . . . digesting, after the tissues of the digestive tract have no defenses against them and . . ."

"Embalming does a lot for us to be remembered by, too," he cut in, insisting, "I said I'd seen untended dead go from waxy pale to mottled frostbite cherry, plum, and fly-blown black. Mayhaps that's a part of the fear we layfolk feel for your magic. It may be we just don't enjoy being reminded of the day, the inevitable day, we get to rot, our ownselves, unless we let some stranger stick us up our dead rear entrances with a trocar and pump us full of cranberry poison."

She put her head back down, sobbing he was just like all the men a girl like her got to meet. So he put a hand softly on one heaving shoulder to insist right back, "I'm telling you the why of it, not the right or wrong of it, Miss Alice. No man with a lick of sense would throw a gal like you out of bed for eating crackers there. But you ought to get out more if you want to socialize with folk of the male or she-male persuasion who ain't as used to Mister Death as you are. That's who that poor

81

Rosa Moreno was really out to snub this evening, Miss Alice. She snubbed you, instead, because Mister Death don't care whether he had welcome or not. So most of us get scared of the inevitable and have to lash out at somebody who *might* care!"

She sat up, wanly, to dab at her eyes with one corner of her fresh apron as she sighed and said, "You remind me of my father. He used to say soldiers did ugly things and sang pretty songs to keep from thinking too hard about tomorrow. Do you really want a slice of my pie, Custis?"

He said he sure did, knowing better than to mention that big plate of migas or the other way her offer could be taken by some cuss less couth.

Her tuna pie had turned out grand enough for him to accept a generous second helping, along with more coffee, as they somehow wound up in her front sitting room on one big overstuffed leather settee, stuffing themselves with pie and tangy mousetrap cheese from the bitty mahogany table that seemed to go with such otherwise comfortable furniture.

When she asked him, with his mouth full, whether he'd like to pick out a coffin for Ramona from her showroom next door, Longarm had to wash the cheese and pie down before he got to chuckle and say, "There you go again. I told you before that first things came first. Now that you've fixed her so she'll keep a few days I'd like to wait and see if anyone within miles of El Paso ever knew her. Meanwhile, are you in the habit of bringing up the subject of coffins whilst sparking on a settee just at twilight?"

She blinked and softly demanded, "Oh? Are you sparking with me, Custis Long?"

To which he could only honestly reply, "I ain't sure. I'll allow it sounds ridiculous if you'll allow you ought to practice just a few of the social graces. Don't you ever entertain gentlemen callers who ain't in no market for no coffins, Miss Alice?"

It developed she hadn't had all that many. As he understood her sad story, told over more of those almond cakes and another wedge of cheese as the original platter gave out, Alice had been a sort of tomboy schoolgirl with a sickly mother when her then-young dad, ranch raised and not educated enough to rate a commission in even a rebel army, had lit out with Hood's Texas Brigade in search of glory but learned a trade, instead, planting many a hero of both sides in various stages of death and decay. Meanwhile his wife back home had managed to get killed by the cholera instead of the damnyankees and for a spell, there, a twelve-year-old child had been put through a rough time, waiting on tables and fending off advances she wasn't sure she understood until the great day her daddy came marching home, whipped, but with a way more profitable trade than punching cows.

He'd naturally taught his only child the same skills and Alice allowed she'd been happy enough at it until her dad had died a few years back and she'd suddenly noticed how gloomy a house without another soul, upstairs at night, could feel.

When pressed, she admitted a swain or more might have noticed she wasn't bad-looking and had her own business. More than one of them had been in the same business, but, being she-male, she just hadn't fancied any of them. The ones she had all wanted to take her away from all this by selling her business cheap, lock, stock, and barrel.

She hadn't been that she-male and Longarm agreed a man with so little respect for a lady's chosen career would be likely to abuse her in other ways, once he'd cleaned her out.

It was commencing to look as if he was sharing the gathering dusk on a cozy settee with a virgin in her late twenties and there were some responsibilities no man wanted to take on if he had any sense at all. So he set aside his coffee cup as best he could in such tricky light as he considered a graceful exit and, with any luck at all, a part of El Paso with more action whilst he awaited permission to get out of such dull surroundings entire.

Women were funny that way. He'd never yet figured out the way they knew a gent wasn't getting set to make a play for them, or why they resisted a man deciding for himself with as much determination. He hadn't even said he was going before she suddenly made a grab for his thigh in the dark, mayhaps grabbing a tad higher than planned, as she pleaded, "Don't go, Custis. It's still early and I've been so lonely. I mean, even before the nasty shock I got this evening."

He gently moved her hand a few inches, lest she notice what a mind of its own his pecker had, as he quietly said, "I put away more of that pie than you did, Miss Alice, and it could be later than you think. I got to find a better place to spend the rest of the night than that ranger station or a hotel that Fool Killer knows about, so . . ."

"Stay here," she cut in, firmly adding, "Nobody else could be expecting you to stay here. There's a lot to be said for shacking up for the night in a haunted house with the neighborhood ghoul, you know!"

So there it was, plain and simple, unless she was talking dumb as some teasing virgins were inclined to, bless their confounding souls. So he said, "I ain't as worried about your ghoulish nature as much as I am your, ah, natural history, Miss Alice."

She moved her hand back where it had been, and sort of squeezed, as she calmly replied, "I'm a lot more frustrated than inexperienced or, for God's sake, frigid, and would you please stop calling me a damned *Miss*? I know I've never been married, dammit to hell, but that's not saying I don't have feelings, is it?"

Since she was feeling him indeed there seemed no better course for a gent in such an awkward position but to reel her in and feel her right back as their lips met, hot and hungry as old friends who'd been missing one another a spell. He was more delighted than surprised to discover she had nothing on under her thin cotton skirts. From the way she responded he could tell she expected him to just shove her backward and mount her aboard that settee with his own three piece suit and gun rig on. But now that he understood her better he just finished undressing her, swept her naked and sweetly clinging form up with him as he rose, fully dressed, and demanded directions to the nearest damned bed.

She steered him to her bed chamber on the same floor, laughing part of the way and sobbing he was so masterful the rest of the way. But once he'd plopped her across a four poster, shucked his own duds, and lay down to join her, Alice was on top, growling at him like a wildcat in heat as she impaled herself on his full erection and demanded even more penetration.

They found out a sweet spell later he could get it in her even deeper from behind, with his feet planted wide on her bedroom rug while she took him dog-style with her spine arched, whimpering for yet more.

A man could only try and it sure beat pissing, but he wondered as he thrust in and out, that way, whether those head doctors over in Vienna Town who'd started to study such notions would agree with him that a gal in the habit of shoving tools way the hell up inside of folks might get to sort of daydreaming, working alone while as lonely as she'd said.

Longarm was a tall man in every way and many an other-wise right friendly gal had asked him to take it easy, not anywheres near as deep as old Alice seemed to need it. But he finally got her to say Uncle, and come, with her slender hips on two pillows and the head of his old organ grinder hitting bottom with every stroke.

Later, as they were sharing a smoke and some more friendly love play, she told him that other gal, downstairs, had been ravaged up her ass as well. He said he wasn't surprised. Then, since she was the one who'd brought that touchy subject up again, Longarm blew a thoughtful smoke ring at the barely visible ceiling and confided, "I'd have a better handle on the sort of cuss I'm hunting if I had a better grasp of why any man might prefer his love toys all the way dead."

She began to toy some more with his love muscles as she seemed more willing, now, to confide, "It's a problem we all have but don't like to talk about in the funeral trade, darling. Nobody who takes his or her skills seriously would consider such a thing, of course, but, well, we do have to hire help for as little as we can manage and you don't get much in the way of brains or even common sense unless you can afford to pay for it."

He let her have a drag as he casually assumed that old helper she'd fired had been caught in the act with a corpse. But she said she doubted the old gent who'd started out working for her father could have gotten it up.

He didn't want to know how she'd surmised this. He said he'd take her word on that and asked her to tell him about the sort of low life who *might* abuse a dead woman that way.

She said, "I'm not sure abuse is the word, dear. It's probably the simple fact that she can't possibly complain, no matter what he does to her, that the necrophiliac finds so exciting."

She gave his far-from-dead tool a playful tug as she teasingly added, "Lord knows one can't expect much *action* from a cadaver."

He reached across her to get rid of the fool cheroot and give her some action back with his once-more-free hand as he muttered, half to himself, "Yep, lack of resistance to one's advances, soft or savage, might inspire a really shy cuss who can't get along in bed with a live or, hell, even dead-drunk woman."

86

He began to finger this living doll's moist clit as he asked her professional opinion on such moisture as they might be talking about, down yonder, with the she-male partner dead.

Alice repressed a shudder and said, "Ouch. I suppose it would work if the man used plenty of hair grease, or spit. A *live* woman being raped doesn't lubricate the way I seem to, right now, you rascal!"

So he took advantage of her natural lubrication and shot some of his own love juice up her to make things even slicker.

So they screwed, smoked, and even dozed off a time or more in one another's arms until they both decided they were hungry, along about ten P.M. That inspired her to hop out of bed and fry plenty of ham and eggs in just her apron for a late supper served in bed.

As they ate by candlelight, bare assed atop the covers, she got around to how long this magic was likely to continue. Women were always fucking up the magic by examining it too close.

Longarm went on chewing long enough to choose his words before he gulped and wistfully told her, "Nothing lasts forever, as a gal in your line of work must have noticed by now. But I wasn't fixing to run off to no rose-covered hideout with another gal just yet. I'm here to help solve a mystery that has us all purely stumped and I sure would like to know more about that gal downstairs."

Alice nodded eagerly and said, "I left her uncovered, to show you as soon as you came back, but I guess we got distracted. Would you like to see her, now?"

Longarm swallowed more ham and eggs before he assured her he'd already peered in on the late Ramona Taylor and added, "It's my professional hope someone who knew her better than us will come forward to view your masterpiece. For if it turns out she was fibbing about being known in these

87

parts we got to backtrack her tangled trail as well. How long will she, ah, be all right down there?"

Alice sipped some of the coffee she'd brewed as well, with the apparent intention of staying awake a spell, before she decided, "It might be less distressing to her loved ones if they view her remains within the week. Knowing what you wanted, and having been taught the trade by a war veteran, I embalmed her in the military fashion with a good four pounds of arsenic salts as well as strong formalin. Sixty instead of forty percent formaldehyde."

Longarm quietly agreed a week sounded about right. He knew many a lad buried at Gettysburg or Arlington lay in better shape than your average Egyptian pharaoh, after all this time, thanks to the heroic measures Graves Registration had taken to ship 'em en masse without stinking up the whole country.

He sipped some bitter black coffee to cut the green taste in his mouth as he resisted the temptation to warn a gal who likely knew her business that some localities had started to forbid the use of arsenic embalming because of the way it could cover up a murder.

Nobody thought the late Ramona Taylor had died of arsenic poisoning. So now, while she'd slowly turn to cordovan shoe leather over the next few weeks or months, she'd never stink, and any fool bugs who messed with her remains would be in for a fatal surprise.

Alice was asking him what he'd meant by a tangled backtrail.

He explained, "That Fernando Nash I told you about earlier works better than anyone else who was there for the disgusting crimes against that Arapaho Annie. Sex fiends do play copycat and it's not too tough to picture another maniac with the same bad habits attacking another gal entire a good six hundred miles away from the scene of the first crime."

Alice nodded but demanded, "What difference does it make whether the second victim was really from El Paso or not?"

He said, "Miss Ramona got on the same train as me up in Denver, meaning she, like the late Arapaho Annie, was known for certain up that way. Both were pretty. I've reason to suspect both tended to be flirty eyed, whether they meant it or not. So let's say some poor twisted soul who don't respond to flirty eyes the way most of us leering rascals do, worked up some twisted passion for both the so-called laundress and a footloose lady I really don't know beans about. Do you see how tough that might make it to hang even one of the killing, on the only logical suspect we have?"

She did. She marveled, "That would mean the girl downstairs had been followed, all the way down here, by someone too crazy for me to even imagine!"

He shrugged his bare shoulders and said he'd been unable to come up for a reason to slap leather on a man who'd only asked if a fool newsstand was still open.

Then Alice set their tray aside, lay back across the covers, and opened her thighs, as wide as they could go. So Longarm lost interest in other duties for a spell and that black coffee turned out to have been a grand notion.

But later, as he'd warned her, even the candle gave out and as he lay there staring up in the darkness with her head nestled on his bare shoulder while her soft snores stirred the hairs on his chest, Longarm got back to thinking about less pleasant recent events and, whilst that sure beat speculating on how long forever could be or how high might up go, he simply couldn't begin to put even a loco pattern together.

But he had to try. So he started by agreeing any cuss apt to gun any man at any time for no sensible reason was apt to do most anything to a woman without reasoning it out all that much.

He grimaced in the dark as he unthinkingly hugged warm naked flesh closer to his side, thinking, "But why? Even if a cuss was too shy to get it up with a downright whore like Arapaho Annie, wouldn't it feel better if a gal was only knocked out instead of downright dead and likely shitty betwixt the legs?"

He started to picture the dead girl down below the way she'd been left by her killer and drew back from the disgusting thoughts such pictures could inspire, the way any halfway decent man draws back from picturing his sister, or mother, taking it dog-style or even taking a crap. For some mental pictures are better left unpictured lest they lead to unthinkable thoughts.

But Longarm was paid to try and put his own mind inside the head of others inclined to think unthinkable thoughts. She let the dead, abused but still disturbingly attractive body of Ramona Taylor drift back into mental view and . . . Right, she had crapped a mite on the pillows under her upthrust hips and Alice had said she'd been sodomized as well as raped.

Before or after?

After was the only way that worked in a hotel filled with other guests. So, *bueno,* who could get it up for even a pretty corpse?

Longarm knew the killer had. Might all those bite marks mean a time working up enough passion? Or had the asshole enjoyed himself so much it had made him go wild with passion?

Longarm tried to picture himself in bed like this, alone, with that girl downstairs posed the same way, as naked, as the live one he had handier. Ramona had been pretty. She was still pretty, and he'd dammit missed out on what he'd been sure would be a sure thing. So let's say he had the chance, right now, whilst her flesh was still soft and. . . . He had to cuss, and then he laughed.

When Alice asked, half asleep, what was so funny, he could only tell her, "It ain't funny. It's insane. The son of a bitch has to be crazy as a loon as well as nasty as a wolverine!"

Chapter 10

Next morning, after a swell breakfast and Alice atop her kitchen table instead of an after-coffee smoke, Longarm got dressed to go see what else might have come up overnight.

At the telegraph office he found messages from both Billy Vail and the War Department. Great minds seemed to run in the same fool channels. The army wasn't ready to let Fernando Nash off the hook, but they weren't about to put him on trial until the disturbingly similar killing of a lady he couldn't have killed could be solved or, failing that, forgotten.

Meanwhile the army meant to hold Nash at nearby Fort Bliss and Billy Vail's orders were to make sure nobody working for Uncle Sam got back-shot in the process.

So he ambled on over to the El Paso Jail, mulling over the not-too-detailed orders as he went with the current. He'd already wired his home office nobody had been exactly back-shot. But of course that had been before someone had spanged a rifle at him over there on railroad property. So why quibble about the bad habits of a mad dog? Longarm suspected the current fame of Henry McCarty, McArthy, or Billy the Kid stemmed from the harmless-looking rascal's habit of shooting at folk frontways, sideways, and just as often from the back. But of course, all bets were off if that rifleman he'd met in the rail yards was some other son of a bitch entire!

It happened that way, he'd sometimes learned the hard way. For any man who packed a badge for any length of time made enemies and he'd put a lot of folk in jail, or the ground, in the six or eight years he'd been riding for the Justice Department.

He paused near the jail to light up in advance lest he wind up having to offer so damned many. As he shook out the match he swore silently at the worse pests who could slow a busy lawman down with their own private grudges. In those Ned Buntline romances about a West Longarm had yet to see, the villains came at the hero way more tidy than in real life. Did wild pistol play in the dark add up to broad-day rifle sniping on the part of the same villain?

First things coming first, he moseyed on over to the jail to see if anyone there had any thoughts on transferring the prisoner out to the army guardhouse at the nearby fort. The first thing the El Paso desk sergeant told him was, "Jesus H. Christ, we've searched high and we've searched low for you since late yesterday, Longarm! Where in hell have you been?"

Longarm smiled thinly and said, "It was more like Heaven to me than any hell. But let's not get into my personal life. What's all this excitement? I told you boys yesterday afternoon why that livery bay tore on home to its stall without me. Don't tell me someone's made even an educated guess as to where the son of a bitch fired from?"

The desk sergeant didn't. He told Longarm, "Your dry gulcher or someone with the same bad habits fired on yet another lawman after sundown. This time he used a pistol with more fatal results. Gunned a deputy sheriff riding for Doña Ana County just up the valley and nailed him smack through the heart, like them others. Naturally our jurisdiction don't extend across the New Mexico line but just as naturally we told 'em we'd pass the word on to you federal men working on El Matador de los Bobos. They're sure that's who done it and they're puzzled as all get-out!"

Longarm said he could hardly blame them but that he was there to talk about transferring Fernando Nash. That was when the El Paso man told him the army had hauled Nash away the night before by ambulance wagon, escorted by a full platoon of mounted dragoons.

Longarm blew a thoughtful smoke ring before deciding, "I reckon that leaves me free to see if I can scout up some sign. Las Cruces would be the county seat of Doña Ana, right?"

The desk sergeant nodded and said, "That's where the most recent killing took place. In the crap house of the railroad depot, there. The army's already sent a military police team up there, along with that young corporal who might know the killer on sight."

Longarm could have voiced some doubts about that. But he never. It was possible Corporal Finch might not mistake someone who just wouldn't fit at all for a shadowy shootist he'd glimpsed, at least, in bum light.

Consulting his mental timetable for the Denver & Rio Grande he decided, "There wasn't no northbound passenger train the cuss who shot at me could have hopped in time to shoot folk in a shithouse in Las Cruces just after dark. But now that I think back I do recall a switch engine, way across the yards, making up a way-freight that could have pulled out around sunset and Las Cruces would be, what, an hour's run?"

The other lawman pursed his lips and allowed, "A way-freight'd get there slower, but not that much slower. So, sure, let's say he saw he'd missed you, knew that yard would soon be crawling with El Paso P.D., and hopped a boxcar north. That would put him in the right place for a railroad station shooting at a time, I fancy. Say he didn't feel he looked hobo

94

enough to fit in, so he dropped off at the first main stop to change to a passenger train. Then . . ."

"Then he shot a lawman who wasn't after him?" Longarm objected, adding, "To avoid attracting attention to himself?"

The El Paso lawman shrugged And said, "We've established him as a homicidal maniac. Witnesses in the D and RG waiting room recall his latest victim better. The local deputy was better known. So a heap of locals noticed him going into the crap house, after which they heard one shot and noticed this one stranger coming out, striding neither slow nor fast as he simply faded off into the night."

When Longarm asked what the cuss might have looked like, the desk sergeant pointed out he hadn't been there. Longarm thought about trains some more and decided, "I got plenty of time to make the next northbound. But I'd best get cracking if I aim to leave in a tidy state."

Suiting actions to his words he went back to the ranger station to find nobody had stolen his saddle and possibles or sent a Texas Ranger up New Mexico way, as interesting as they'd found the news of yet another killing.

Toting his load first to the closer railroad depot and checking it with the baggage clerk for now, Longarm retraced his steps to Alice's, making sure he had the checkbook from a saddlebag.

Alice seemed happy and horny to see him again so soon. When he told her he had to run up to Las Cruces and aimed to get up to date with her on Ramona's funeral expenses Alice gasped, "Oh, no, how could you ask me to take money from you, *now*?"

He sat down at the kitchen table and got to work with a fountain pen from the same saddlebag as he snorted in annoyance and growled, "Shoot, girl, I couldn't afford to pay for other services on my salary. If you ever decided to sell your sweet ass it would be worth way more than Miss

95

Lillie Langtry charges that Prince of the Wales. I got to settle up for the swell job you done on that poor little thing you got down in your cellar and, well, we ought to consider storage fees as well, seeing I'd like you to keep her till I get back."

She brightened, assured him she'd never go dog-style with the fat old Prince of Wales at any price, and asked how long he might be away from her loving arms.

He told her truthfully he didn't know, explaining, "If I cut a trail I generally follow it, as far as it leads for as long as it takes. If I ain't back, and if no kith or kin have come forward in . . . let's give 'em another seventy-two hours, you may as well plant the poor gal out back of that Papist mission you suggested. For she did say she was at least half Spanish."

Then he asked exactly how much he owed her for all she'd done so far and added, "Don't forget storage fees for at least three more days, if you're willing. I mean, I can see how a lady living alone might feel uneasy about such matters."

Alice said, "Pooh, I told you I embalmed her army style and if you're talking about the *notion* of bodies in the basement, it goes with the family business. Does twenty dollars for the embalming and four dollars for that funeral dress sound too steep, darling?"

He chuckled and said, "Not for army style. Last time I buried anyone out of my own pocket, up Durango way, it ran me sixty bucks and a contribution to the church. Why don't I just make this out for an even hundred and that way you can handle anything extra that might come up before I can get back?"

He didn't think she wanted to be reminded a lawman didn't come back every time. She said he was offering her as much as many a family head made in two months. He said he'd noticed that and so she could give him back any change he might have coming the next time he passed this way.

She said she and Miss Ramona would sure be waiting and that inspired her to insist he follow her downstairs to see how good she was at everything she put serious effort into.

Curious despite a certain natural distaste he'd always felt for the pregnant stillness of his old acquaintance, Mister Death, Longarm followed Alice down to the cellar, where Ramona now lay under a drop cloth that made her seem, if anything, more spooky. But when Alice whisked the cloth from the dead girl's calm and once more pretty features Longarm found himself nodding a silent wistful howdy. One had to look close to notice a sort of bronze sheen under the face powder and nicely applied hints of healthy color. Alice noticed, too. She sighed and said, "I wish there was some way of preserving the tissues without darkening them."

Longarm said, "Well, her being part Mex helps and, as I said, she'll be planted by her kin or by us within a few days. You're sure she won't be a bother, laid out where she is?"

Alice covered the cadaver again, explaining she'd just move the poor dear if any unexpected business came their way, unless he'd like to choose a coffin and help her box the dead girl before he left.

He shook his head and said, "Two reasons. Any kin who do come forward might feel I was uppity and I got a train to catch."

So she asked if he had to catch his train this very minute and he fibbed and said he did before she could get him back in bed to part friendlier. It wasn't as if he was tired of screwing her. He simply knew how tough it was to stop, with such a wildcat, once a man got started. So he kissed her, French, and told her she'd pay for that last remark as soon as he got back.

Then he left before she could change his mind.

That actually left him with a tad more time on his hands than he really needed. So as long as he was moping about, downtown, he followed a few loose ends that led nowhere important.

El Paso P.D. seemed as sure as Alice Fischel that the old drunk she'd fired, known to his pals in the drunk tank as Reb Durler, had been innocent as far as the late Ynez Gomez was concerned. Peeping kids spying an old boozer washing the nubile naked cadaver of the unfortunate beauty had doubtless distorted such a thunder-gasting sight into something even wilder. It was generally agreed something had happened to poor old Reb during the war, but that sex mania had hardly been it and, even if he had been screwing the pretty Gomez gal's dead body, that time, he'd been in the drunk tank, as usual, the night those first two soldiers had been gunned by the likely rapist of the late Ramona Taylor.

By the time Longarm figured out a few other ways a cuss some Mex kids had down as a corpse screwer could rate at least the usual grilling, it was time he really caught that northbound.

So he did and, by passenger coach, at least, Las Cruces was the hour up the line that he'd figured.

Knowing this, he'd kept his saddle and possibles with him, in a forward coach car, lest he lose track of his stop at the bar in the club car. The tracks followed the muddy Rio Grande on their left, running north and south up this way before swinging east at El Paso to form part of the U.S.-Mexican border. Everything over to the right was sun-dried grass and dusty spinach-green mesquite with some prickle-pear hither and yon. That reminded him of tuna pie and tuna pie reminded him of some mighty fine pussy he'd passed up on, fool that he was, now that he'd rested up some.

Then they were passing the more interesting but not that interesting foothills of the sun-baked Organ Mountains. So he knew he'd be getting off soon. Just as he knew, or sensed, someone was staring hard at the nape of his neck.

Whipping around at such times could get a cuss shot, or make a fool of him if he was throwing down on a kid who was simply curious about big hats worn Colorado Crush. So Longarm rose casually, as if to get at his overhead saddle, and rummaged a handful of nothing out of a saddlebag before he glanced back, as if at his seat instead of every damned seat in the car behind it.

It was that ugly old gal with the wedding band and great body. She'd ridden down from Denver that night with him. She'd checked into that same hotel with him. Now she seemed to riding back the way they'd come, still boring holes in him with her smouldering Apache eyes. It was enough to make a man ask a strange lady what in the fuck she was up to.

But he never. It was a free country. The old bat had a right to go back where she'd apparently come from after finishing whatever she'd had to do in El Paso and he'd be getting off in the next few minutes. So there was no sense adding another lunatic to his list of suspects.

It didn't matter who she was or what she'd been up to, as long as she kept on going when they got to Las Cruces. For while it was possible for even a pretty gal to dress up like a man and shoot a gun, no gal could have come in Ramona's dead body, front or back, and the most recent shooting had taken place in Las Cruces whilst that definite she-male back yonder had definitely been in El Paso, like himself.

Thinking about her in the hall of the Eagle, with her kimono wide open, made him miss Alice some more, and admire her way better as well. The poor cuss who'd put that ring on that other old gal's finger had to be suffering some confused feelings below the belt as well, thinking about confused feelings. Kissing a face that ugly would surely hurt like hell, even though he now knew she was built just grand where no man could tell before he'd swapped spit with a face that could stop a clock.

He was glad when she didn't get off with him at Las Cruces. He'd have had to question her if she had and, try as he might, he found he just couldn't help considering that a man wouldn't have to look at her face, going at that hour-glass figure dog-style.

Since Las Cruces was the county seat, the *town* of Doña Ana being a smaller flag stop up the line, Longarm didn't have far to go and they sure seemed happy to see him at the sheriff's department near the county courthouse. After that things started going to pot. For, as the local and army investigators had already established before his arrival, the killer had just strode off into the night into thin air, as far as anyone in the county-entire could determine.

Ben Wilke, the local deputy shot in the shithouse, had been a likable popular cuss. So even Mex vaqueros off the surrounding cow spreads had fanned out at moonrise to cut any trails such a *cagon* might have left.

They'd cut none, of course. No livery in Las Cruces had hired a mount to any mysterious stranger. Nobody from town was missing a mount and nobody with a lick of sense *walked* out across semidesert with armed and dangerous men who knew the country riding back and forth across it in a searching pattern.

When Longarm asked, they wearily confirmed they'd checked out all the flops from rooming houses to hobo jungles a transient had half a chance of holing up in with the streets aswarm right after early evening gunplay.

Longarm was saved some personal legwork when it developed the experienced county lawmen had taken down and typed up depositions from every soul who'd been anywhere near the railroad depot at the time. They hadn't let anyone board a train, either way, before they'd had a good long talk with everyone.

So, in sum, as Longarm had already been told, the late Ben Wilke had entered the D&RG waiting room just after nightfall, apparently with nothing but a call to nature in mind as he strode into the gent's room at the far end of the waiting room. Nobody had been able to say exactly how long he'd been in there. Nobody had cared until they all heard the same shot. One shot. Most agreed a .45 sounded right and that was what the coroner had dug out of the dead deputy that morning. Descriptions varied some, albeit none importantly, as to the stranger everyone saw coming out, moments later. He hadn't volunteered any comments about the gun smoke wafting out the doorway after him and nobody had seen fit to question him about it, which was likely why so many of 'em were still alive, in the opinion of one Doña Ana deputy.

He told Longarm, "They say El Matador de los Bobos only kills folk who talk to him, see?"

Another deputy snorted dubiously and asked, "What do you reckon that gal he kilt the other night in El Paso said to him? Stop?"

Longarm allowed he was more interested in what the late Ben Wilke might have said in the shithouse to inspire such a rude response. When a Doña Ana rider said nobody knew because nobody had gotten up the nerve to go look until the stranger had vanished into the night and poor Ben had lay dead on the tiles for a spell, alone, Longarm said he'd just read that and asked when and where anyone there had seen that army team he was supposed to back up.

A Doña Ana man said the two officers and four enlisted men had fanned out to scout up witnesses that the county might have failed to question. Longarm agreed army officers could talk like that.

Meanwhile the courthouse clock outside was clanging fit to bust. When it finished counting to eleven and fell silent again Longarm said, "It's fixing to get hotter before it gets cooler and even a tin soldier gets to eat around noon. So where would I feed a mixed crew of officers and enlisted men, here in Las Cruces, if I was in command?"

101

After some consultation the locals decided on the Posada del Rio because it was a big old ramblesome wayside inn on the edge of town with plain and fancy separate dining rooms and, hell, a stand-up cantina facing the corral if a traveler was in a hurry.

So that was where Longarm headed next, lugging his damned old saddle just in case. The mostly 'dobe structures of Las Cruces started spreading apart as one left the center of town and he'd already been caught out on an open field of fire without his old Winchester, thanks to acting lazy under a dry country sun.

When he'd finally trudged all the dusty way to the Posada del Rio he found it much as described, albeit a mite more squatty and ground hugging than Anglos might have built a wayside inn with that many rooms.

There was a sign, printed in English and dangled under the tiles of the front veranda, that steered him to the right doorway to the main lobby. He still had to ding a brass bell on the dark deserted desk and he'd put his heavy load down on the tile floor before, at last, a plump but pretty gal of about thirty or less, allowing for how some mestizas matured if they got more to eat than usual, came out of a dinky doorway, surly as anything until she saw him standing there and decided to smile, after all.

He howdied her politely, identified himself, and told her what he was doing there. She looked sort of let down, sighed, and told him if he didn't want a room he could find plenty to eat or drink by simply stepping through either archway, left or right, leading to their sit-down or stand-up facilities. When he asked about the army team she shrugged and said nobody but him had pestered her all morning. He said he'd ask the other help about them but went on to say, "All of us are interested in a tall dark stranger who'd have been looking for a night's shelter in the recent past, ma'am. I'm sure you'd recall anyone like that hiring a room from you, early or late, last night?"

She sighed and said, "I am called Lizeta, and perhaps a dozen county deputies and as many vaqueros have already asked me that. It was a very long night, but not at all interesting, and I thought I was going to be able to catch up on my beauty rest at last, until just now, eh?"

He said he was sorry he'd disturbed her and suggested she go on back to bed. It wouldn't have been polite to ask if she'd been in bed alone, just now. But he had noticed most gals wiped off their makeup entire if they meant to sleep alone.

As she vanished through that bitty door to go back to bed with her own business, Longarm toted his McClellan and such through the archway to his right and found the stand-up cantina he'd been told about at the far end of a corridor lined with squatty oaken doors. There were two reasons 'dobe architecture along the border tended to hug the ground closer than Anglo frame. 'Dobe tended to settle as it aged and border folk were inclined to be shorter than either Anglo Saxons or pure Spanish folk. Most of their Indian blood was Uto-Aztec because that particular breed of small boned natural survivor had always survived best in an often pretty but never forgiving country.

The barkeep behind the otherwise deserted bar was an overweight mestizo as well. He said Longarm could see for himself no soldiers had come in yet. Longarm ordered a cerveza and asked if he could leave his McClellan there whilst he scouted the dining rooms for the army crew. The barkeep allowed it would be safer behind the bar, with him, than down there by the brass rails and spittoons.

As Longarm handed it over the polished oak bar to him he added they expected way more business than usual, once all the riders from the more distant ranchos drifted in to search for that son of a bitch who'd shot Ben Wilke.

Longarm didn't have the heart to say he doubted the son of a bitch could be out on that dry range on foot. He just drifted out with his beer schooner to see if that army crew could be in another part of the posada.

They weren't. He went back to the cantina and ordered one more cerveza. When the barkeep offered to needle it for him with a dash of tequila Longarm shook his head and said, "Not before noon and some grub down yonder to soften the blow. I'm officiously on duty. I got to see where them officers mean to eat before I order my own noon dinner. Left to my druthers I reckon I'd settle for that stand-up cantina down to the far end. I just now smelled a pot of long-simmered chili con carne that gave me a hard-on. It ain't easy to get chili con carne made just right this close to the border."

The barkeep said he guessed they made their chili hotter than most sissy Texans and Longarm said that was what he meant. But he didn't go into his Darwinian notions about Tex-Mex grub evolving from a contest betwixt heroic pepper chewers, Tex or Mex. He just hauled out his watch to make sure his stomach growls were correct and muttered, "The damned peace-time army always eats at noon. I fear I've been directed the wrong damned distance with a heavy load and the sun not getting any cooler as it keeps on rising!"

It was just after high noon as he finished his drink and went back to the cantina at the far end. The counter was higher, lest customers spill soup on their vests as they inhaled it standing up. But otherwise Mex-built stand-ups were a lot alike. The combined cook's helper and counterman was skinny as a rail, as if to prove not everyone with Uto-Aztec blood put on weight as soon as they were allowed to eat as much as other humans. Longarm didn't doubt the skinny Mex ate plenty of their swell chili con carne. For anyone who wouldn't have wanted to would have had to be coming down with something and the skinny cuss looked healthy enough.

104

Their tamales smelled swell, too, so Longarm ordered a couple of them for dessert. Tamales weren't at all sweet but they reminded him of pastry and Mex attempts at sweet pastry didn't do half as much for him.

There was chicory in the coffee. But it was good strong stuff and he figured they were trying to be fancy French instead of sly. He'd just about finished and he was starting to contemplate that long trudge back to the center of town with that fool McClellan when he heard hoofbeats outside and knew at least half a dozen riders were either anxious about something or in the habit of mistreating their mounts this close to siesta time.

After some hustle, bustle, and shouting back and forth, a young shavetail spied Longarm at the counter through an open window and called out, "He's back here, Lieutenant!"

So Longarm wasn't too surprised when a somewhat older first john clomped in to join him, with his shavetail and a quartet of enlisted men in tow. All six of 'em had on M.P. brassards as well as six-guns and, for Pete's sake, cavalry sabers.

One of the enlisted men was the familiar Corporal Finch. Longarm had never laid eyes on any of the others and he was just as glad when the first john introduced himself as a Lieutenant Robinson and tossed in his wartime brevet rank. Lots of old boys who wouldn't have made a pimple on a field grade officer's ass had made it to Brevet Major by the end of the war.

The overage-in-grade Lieutenant Robinson told Longarm they'd been told where he might be by those county deputies and so they'd picked up a spare mount for him, as well, from the sheriff's remuda. Longarm said he was glad nobody expected him to walk any further but still asked where they all might be headed.

Robinson said, "North, to the rail stop at San Marcial. Our man has struck again. This time he may be wounded and his latest victim not only survived but shot it out with the villain in broad daylight. So what are you waiting for? Let's go!"

Longarm didn't want to make a leader look like a total asshole in front of his own men, so he chose his words carefully and still pissed Robinson off when he quietly suggested, "San Marcial is over seventy miles up the river, Lieutenant."

Robinson nodded stiffly and demanded, "Did you think I was in the habit of charging blindly off across desert range, Deputy Long? I know exactly where San Marcial is and we can lop off a good ten to fifteen miles by following a straighter wagon trace."

Longarm nodded and said, "I've been over it. The Mexicans call that stretch of their old wagon route La Jornada del Muerto. It's a heap safer, now, what with the railroad having drilled a couple of tube wells betwixt hither and yon. But, speaking of railroads, has it occurred to you even a slow freight would cover that whole hard ride in less than three hours, Lieutenant?"

Robinson showed him why they'd ordered him to pitch in and offer the military police a hand by insisting, stiffly, "I already asked about that. There won't be another northbound train through Las Cruces this side of sundown. Something about them preferring to cross that desert stretch after dark whenever possible. Meanwhile, I prefer not to waste a whole day down here with that killer still at large up in San Marcial!"

Longarm suggested just the two of 'em step out in the hallway for a few words in private. Robinson must have thought Longarm had secret instruction, for he followed him out of earshot of his men with no argument.

The argument started after Longarm told him, privately, "You're an asshole, no offense. San Marcial would be a hard day's ride if you were starting at dawn along New England byways on a cool spring morning. If we could cover half La

106

Jornada del Muerto before that train you just mentioned passed us we'd still have to make camp to keep from killing our horses, with that train passing out the far side of San Marcial before we got us a good fire going!"

Robinson said, "I can't waste a whole afternoon here in Las Cruces doing nothing, dammit!"

Longarm soothed, "There's wasting time stupid and there's wasting it sensible, Lieutenant. I'm sure you did a heap of soldiering back in the greenwoods east of the Big Muddy where most of the fighting took place during the war. Out this way you pay more heed to Mother Nature or what the Indians call Wakan Tonka, because by either name it can kill a greenhorn easy as a kid can stomp an ant."

Robinson snapped, "I'll have you know I've covered a hundred miles at a stretch by horseback without anyone stomping me. So get to the damned point!"

Longarm said, simply, "I thought I had. I'm going to enjoy a three or four hour siesta whilst the sun bakes the trails all it wants. Then I'm going to mosey on back to the depot, maybe eat a good supper, and get off that evening train no later than nine in the evening, bright eyed and bushy tailed, whether that killer is still in San Marcial or not. I sure as hell don't mean to give him another day's lead on me whilst I haul ass across the desert on horseback. So you all do whatever you want and mayhaps I'll be there when you finally ride in. Who am I to ask for, up yonder, in the unlikely event I get there ahead of you?"

Robinson smiled thinly despite himself and said, "You won't. I don't like your suggestions at all but I'm not a total idiot and, yes, I do see why you suggested we have this conversation out here in private. Let's get on back to town and find some shady place to sweat that train out."

Longarm said, "This posada hires rooms and the 'dobe walls and thick roof tiles were meant for this here climate,

Lieutenant. So I mean to stay right here, for now, and you were going to tell me who we're supposed to check in with up in San Marcial, weren't you?"

Robinson said, "The county seat would be about twenty miles up the valley. I was told an Undersheriff Sloan is doing what he can in San Marcial, with the help of the Denver and Rio Grande. One of their railroad dicks was the latest victim. A man called Jarlsborg, I believe."

Longarm whistled and asked, "Swede Jarlsborg?"

When Robinson said that sounded right Longarm explained, "Swede Jarlsborg is an old pro with a rep. The Fool Killer's really good with a gun if he shot it out with old Swede and came out ahead!"

Robinson said, "The way I understand it, Jarlsborg thinks he put a round in the moody mystery man they call El Matador So-Forth."

"Fool Killer," Longarm corrected, adding, "If he left on his own feet he came out ahead in a showdown with a gunslick who's usually done way better than average."

Longarm hauled out his pocket watch, consulted it, and swore, "Son of a bitch if time don't flow like a cat shitting through a funnel when a man's got better places to be! I'm tempted to tear off for San Marcial on horseback my ownself. So I'd better see if I can hire us all some shady flops before I do something way more foolish!"

Chapter 11

There seemed three ways to do most anything. There was a right way, a wrong way, and the army way. So Longarm didn't see fit to argue when Lieutenant Robinson sent two privates back to town with all seven ponies, lest anyone miss out on a swell walk back to the railroad depot later on. Like Longarm, the army detail had brought along their own saddles, harnesses, and packs. So Longarm was smart enough to get them to carry his own McClellan and possibles back with them to be checked in at the depot.

The plump but pretty Lizeta looked even more puffy eyed as she sullenly handed out room keys, muttering in Spanish about cheap gringos when Longarm explained the officers meant to siesta solo but that one room would do for the four enlisted men. He told her he'd take a room with a bath for himself, if they had it. So she handed him the key to their one and only honeymoon suite and that adjoining bath looked more like a sink, stall shower, and hole in a corner of the tile floor.

He didn't care. Once he found himself alone behind a squatty locked door he pissed down the hole, hung his gun rig on a bedpost, and shucked all his duds to flop naked across the bed, atop the cotton covers. For the whole point of La Siesta was that it got *hot* in those parts in the afternoon, even that late in the year.

He knew it would get a heap hotter, outside, before things got more reasonable, no earlier than three or four. In here, with the jalousie blinds cutting most of the light and the thick walls and roof tiles soaking up most of the heat, a naked body felt way better as long as no effort beyond breathing was called for.

Outside, more ambitious souls were moving about, bitching in both English and Spanish about anyone loco enough to be running around like a mad dog in this pendejo heat.

He figured they had to be talking about the cuss who'd killed Ben Wilke. He was tempted to thow open the blinds, at least, and tell 'em the son of a bitch had moved on to shoot other unfortunates. But he never. That barkeep had sounded as if he'd sort of counted on the extra trade and old Lizeta had just told him they were the only guests in any of the rooms for hire, at the moment.

He yawned and shut his eyes, knowing he could be facing a long night whether he was tired enough to sleep right now or not. He'd trained himself to catch such sleep as he could get a crack at. It could make up for the extra hours he could push himself when, not if, he really had to.

So he was just dozing off, thinking of tuna pie, when he heard a gentle rapping on his chamber door and then, before he could even ask if it might be a raven, he heard a key twisting in the damned lock.

Hence the plump Lizeta found herself facing a naked man on his bare feet with a .44-40 trained on her as she slipped inside and still shut the door behind her with a thrust of her ample behind. Longarm was much more aware her behind was covered and his wasn't as she said, "Forgive me, one can see

110

this may not have been such a good time for you, but you did say you were a lawman, no?"

He started to cover his fool privates with the gun he'd been using to cover her. But seeing she'd seen all he had to offer, soft, already, he just nodded and said, "I showed you my badge, and now no I have no secrets from you at all, Miss Lizeta. Who might you be calling the law on?"

She said, "I don't know. Like yourself, I have been trying for to catch a few winks during La Siesta. Pero, someone has been trying for to get in my room and I am frightened!"

Longarm moved back to sit on the bed, with his gun hand casually across his naked lap, as he asked her, soothingly, "Are you sure it wasn't just somebody else in the market for a flop? I've been hearing a whole posse of spurred and booted riders outside, Miss Lizeta."

She came over and sat down beside him on the bed, as if the two of them were full-dressed fellow travelers on a train, as she told him, "Most of them have already left. One of those soldados said El Matador de los Bobos has struck again, up in San Marcial, so it makes no sense for to search for him any more around here, eh?"

Longarm agreed that was about the way he and that M.P. detail had it figured and suggested, "Things ought to simmer down any minute and we can all catch a few winks. So, well, it's sure been grand, but . . ."

"Can't I stay here with you until he goes away?" she pleaded, in a little-kid tone.

When he asked who they were talking about she said she figured it had to be a him, trying to get into her room at her, because she wasn't the kind of muchacha who got in bed with other muchachas.

He said he'd noticed she seemed sort of feminized and added he sure felt sleepy. When she suggested they just lie down together and keep one another safe, he started to say something really dumb about preferring to sleep atop the covers, the way he was, when it was this hot. He thought it made more sense to just put his .44-40 back in its holster and suggest she'd feel more comfortable lying beside him if she took her own duds off.

So she did, as if they were old pals and she'd had something such as this in mind from the beginning.

He felt surer she had once he hauled her naked body in against his for a howdy kiss and she grabbed hold of his old organ grinder before he'd worked up the gall to grab anything more than one of her big brown breasts.

In the end, they both agreed the best way to come together in the middle of La Siesta was in the adjoining shower stall, standing at first and then dog-style, all soapy, both ways, with the almost cold water coming down full blast on their slippery sliding hides. She said that was why they called it the honeymoon suite. But of course, when asked, she insisted she'd never done it in here with a guest before.

So Longarm took the rest of her tale with more than a grain of salt when, back on the bed all goosebumped and sharing a smoke, she insisted she really had come tapping on his door because some creepy crawly had been fumbling with first her door latch and then her window shutters.

When he asked whether she'd risked a peek she allowed she had called out, in both Anglo and Mex, before she'd worked up the grit to peek out.

He said he felt flattered she'd come down the hall to him, anyway, after catching nobody at either her chamber door or side window. She said it had seemed more scary at the time and started to play with his pecker some more to teach him not to tease her.

After they'd done it that way, they even caught a few winks of heat-drugged sleep. Then it was time to get up some more and Lizeta said she just couldn't thank him enough for saving her life like so. But he figured the swell farewell blow job was reward enough, whether she'd made up the whole thing or not.

Chapter 12

They naturally dropped by Western Union on their way to the Las Cruces Depot and found they'd been wired orders Longarm found sort of unnatural. He'd already known San Marcial was little more than a cluster of railroad frame and Mex 'dobe around a handy spot to jerk water as the tracks crossed the river on a timber trestle to get at some flatter rolling. He agreed it made sense to run Swede Jarlsborg on up to the county seat at Socorro, where they had real docs instead of the country vet who'd first treated his wound. But after that Longarm insisted it made more sense to start searching for a criminal's trail near the scene of his latest crime.

Lieutenant Robinson had orders to question Swede Jarlsborg, the only witness who'd ever faced El Matador de los Bobos in broad daylight, and that was where, come hell or high water, Robinson and his team meant to get off.

Robinson said it made no mind to him if Longarm wanted to drop off at San Marcial and question the handful of locals who'd just told their undersheriff they hadn't seen shit.

Longarm was tempted. He knew most of the country folk around San Marcial were Mex or Indian and he seemed to get more out of either than your average Anglo lawman. But his own orders were to lend a hand to the soldiers blue and with Robinson in command they could use it.

Their train was a passenger-freight combination that pulled out of El Paso just before sundown and got to Las Cruces in the gloaming. So it was after dark, but not that long after dark, when they stopped to jerk some top-off water for their tender at San Marcial. "Jerk Water" could be literal as well as dismissive for an otherwise pointless railroad stop. At San Marcial it was literal. The train stopped half on and half off the timber trestle spanning the Rio Grande where it ran more deep and narrow betwixt higher banks than usual. Then the engine crew lowered big buckets on long ropes to the brawling surface on the downstream side. Most of the creamy-coffee silt settled to the bottom of the buckets by the time they hauled the otherwise fresh water all the way up. They didn't stay long to replenish that much water for a tender they'd filled to the top in El Paso, earlier. But the idea in semidesert country was to grab soft water wherever you might meet it, so much of the ground water being too hard for a mule, let alone a steamboiler.

That still gave Longarm time enough to step down to the simple open platform at the ass end of the combination where, just as he'd hoped, a dozen-odd locals with nothing better to do stood gaping at the astounding sight of a railroad train standing still.

Lieutenant Robinson hadn't thought it worth the time and effort it took to tear himself away from the bar in the club car. But as Longarm jawed with the neighborly if not too helpful locals he was joined by Corporal Finch and a couple of more curious privates.

They let Longarm do the talking. He asked some of his questions in his simple but sometimes soothing Spanish. He found out neither Finch nor the others knew even basic Spanish when he had to repeat to them that nobody there had seen nothing.

All but one vaquero had heard the shooting, somewhere along about nine that morning. The vaquero had missed out on the fun by being out on the range. Everyone else in a tiny town had counted five or six shots. By the time anyone could figure where they'd come from, Swede Jarlsborg had staggered out of the slot betwixt this loading platform and some cattle chutes one couldn't quite make out from here in this light to tell 'em where he'd just swapped lead with some son of a bitch in black, and that was all anyone there knew.

Then the engineer out on the trestle tooted the "All Aboard" and the out-of-towners had to climb back on and be content with little more than they'd already figured.

Longarm paused on the open platforms betwixt the club car and the coach ahead to enjoy a cool smoke out here where he only had to taste his own tobacco. Corporal Finch was the only one to stay out there with him. Longarm offered him a smoke as well. He figured the kid would tell him what he wanted in his own good time. They'd already established Finch was engaged to marry up with a she-male.

But he didn't smoke. So Longarm put his offer away with a smile and allowed he wished he didn't, either, adding, "It's easy enough to quit, if you put your mind to it. I quit at least twice a year."

Finch had heard it, but he was polite enough to chuckle before he asked, more soberly, "Do you think we're going to catch that crazy cuss who shot good old Sergeant Plummer, Deputy Long?"

Longarm said, "That's what they want us to do. But I follow your drift, old son. I'm sure Lieutenant Robinson means well and to tell the truth it's six of one and half a dozen of the other. I'd have liked to have spent more time poking around back yonder. On the other hand, save for yourself, Swede Jarlsborg, up at the county seat, seems to be the only man on our side who's laid eyes on the Fool Killer and lived!"

116

Finch grimaced and said, "I wish I'd gotten a really good look or, better yet, a *bead* on the corpse-fucking lunatic! But I've had more time to study on that night back at that Eagle Hotel and, well, I got me a couple notions. Only I can't get the lieutenant to listen to me. He says the army don't pay two-stripers to have notions."

Longarm said, "I had a lieutenant like that one time. As I recall the ending it was somewhere near Cold Harbor I strongly advised him to duck and he was staring down disdainsomely at us mere enlisted men when a minny ball went in his one ear and out the other. But I don't mind hearing anyone's notions, Corporal."

So Finch said, "I figure the killer has to be an old army man or at least a man who's been working around army posts. Maybe our own Camp Weld. Wouldn't that account for poor old Plummer knowing him by sight in shitty light? He shot Plummer with an army issue .45 as well!"

Longarm took a thoughtful drag on his cheroot as they rolled on through the night. Then he said, "Plummer was drilled through the heart by a .45. After that a heap of old boys, starting with the Mexican Rurales, favor .45s, albeit they mostly pack the Colt Model '74 or Peacemaker. You ain't come up with that name yet?"

Finch said, "The more I study on it, the less I think Plummer had a chance to really name his killer. You got to understand how *fast* that son of a bitch was!"

Longarm said, simply, "I do. You're forgetting I met up with him or his double, shortly thereafter. I didn't get to address him by name, though."

Finch said, "I don't think Plummer did, neither. I think Plummer just got out something like, say, don't I know you from that time the Sioux riz, and then he was going down and it was my turn to swap lead with the bastard. You know how that turned out. What I been thinking about is that motive everyone says the bastard just don't have. What if he'd just come from killing and raping Ramona Taylor so disgusting, and what if he'd just cleaned up in that gent's bath down our hall and what if . . ."

"If the dog hadn't stopped to shit it might have caught the rabbit," Longarm cut in, adding, "All your what-ifs work just fine. So do a mess of *other* what-ifs. It's tough enough to put a puzzle together when you're working with all the right pieces. Once you start tossing extra what-ifs on the table it can get confounding indeed."

The kid looked so crestfallen Longarm felt obliged to soothe, "Your mention of a Sioux rising could be of some help when and if we get a better line on a suspect or more. Which Sioux rising betwixt Little Crow and Crazy Horse is less important than the possibility of putting the late Sergeant and some damned suspect in the same outfit or on the same post at some damned time during some damned rising. We call that the process of eliminating. We might be able to eliminate say a whisky drummer who just come West and packs a .36. But as to even a lunatic getting all messy on the second floor and going up to the third to wash up, I dunno."

Finch said, "Makes sense to me, picturing a tricky lunatic who planned ahead. You know how dark the upstairs halls at that hotel were, Deputy Long. Nobody would notice a little blood in such dim light and he might have figured nobody would study as hard on any stranger entering or leaving a bath that far from the one on the dead gal's floor, right?"

Longarm sighed and said, "Right but wrong about all them might-haves and what-ifs, again. I can think of as many reasons *not* to wander all over a hotel covered with blood."

He fished out his watch and held it up to the light through the door glass to check their progress by rail as he continued, "I'll give you a what-if. Nobody mentioned blood on the duds of Fernando Nash and he was picked up by los rurales wearing the same outfit he had on when he tore out the gate up at Camp Weld."

Finch suggested Nash could have ravaged Arapaho Annie in the nude, and taken time to wash up in her laundry shed, after.

Longarm nodded and said, "Lots of old boys panic and run blind after a thorough wash-up in private. Whether Nash or the same one who murdered and raped Ramona Taylor abused that Indian laundress is for a court martial to determine. My only point is that *both* gals were likely treated so savage by a blood thirsty asshole who had plenty of time to shuck all his duds after he'd killed 'em."

Finch made a wry face and said, "Everyone keeps saying he made wild love to both of them after they were already dead!"

Longarm said, "Not both, for certain. Ramona Taylor for sure. I got it on good authority she was raped in the ass as well but never felt it. Some old boys just can't take no for an answer and if you kill a gal before you ask, she can't say no, see?"

Finch said he didn't, adding, "I don't think I could even touch my true love with my hand, down there, if she lay downright dead!"

Longarm said, "Well, most of us were brung up to find dead flesh distasteful, unless it's cow, pig, or chicken flesh, least-ways. I got this friend down in El Paso who can't give fresh-baked pastry away because her neighbors know she has to touch the skin of a dead human now and again. Her neighbors make the sign-of-the-cross when she walks by. Then they go back to plucking the gizzard and guts out of the old gray goose they've had hanging in the pantry a spell to get tender. It makes you wonder whether a butcher has trouble getting folk to shake with him, don't it?"

Finch shook his head stubbornly and said, "I don't think I could stick my dong in anything dead, albeit it does sound

119

more comical when you picture it in a dead goose. Doing anything like that to a dead lady somehow sounds more creepy crawly to me!"

Longarm nodded and said, "Welcome to the human race. They call them other gents necrophiliacs because they seem to be a form of maniac. A mania is a loco drive that gets into a body and won't get out, no matter how loco it seems, even to the maniac, until it's been satisfied."

Finch gulped and half murmured, "You mean Nash and that other corpse fucker kill the women they rape because they feel they just *have* to?"

Longarm shrugged and said, "Close enough. Unless someone so slick he has to be loco in another way is out to convince us Nash didn't kill that laundress up at Camp Weld. I don't know how rare really dedicated necrophiliacs might be. But they can't be very common or the rest of us wouldn't find their love lives quite so shocking. We'd best go in and gather our gear, now. They'll be letting us off at the county seat any time, now."

Chapter 13

Socorro sprawled along the west bank of the Rio Grande where it ran through a fairly fertile slot betwixt the Sierra Obscura to the southeast and the foothills of the higher Magdalenas off to the west. Aside from being a railroad stop and the county seat Socorro was in the business of raising stock and produce, mostly cows, goats, corn, and beans. Most of its working population was of Mex or Indian ancestry with the county political machinery run by Anglo newcomers to the valley. The Mexicans had been there before the Mexican War, so they were considered U.S. citizens whether they spoke English or not, as long as they kept their place. As to the Indians, they were mostly Pueblos or Mission Nadene and if there was one thing Anglo and Mex settlers agreed on it was that Indians should either work for good Christians or stay the hell out of their way. So, thanks to that part of New Mexico being run that much like old Mexico, Socorro was lit up festive and most everyone was out in the main plaza enjoying the balmy evening when Longarm and the M.P. detail got off there with their baggage.

Dozens of mean little kids wanted to tote their saddles and

such to competing hotels, of course. But the Socorro sheriff's department had been expecting them, with a buckboard, so the kids were out of luck, albeit not out of things to say about pendejos gringo at a safer distance.

The big-cheese sheriff was off somewheres more important, but the deputies he'd sent said they knew the best posada for the bunch of them to store their saddles and bed down, later, if none of them got lucky. It seemed it was the eve of some fool saint's day and there was nothing like a religious festival to get some señoritas all emotional. Before they could fully explain the charming Paseo Coqueteria further Longarm said he knew how to get laid down this way and asked about Swede Jarlsborg.

They said he was at the same posada, now, having been patched up by their doc and warned to take it easy for a spell. Robinson said he'd felt a lot better as soon as they'd dug a rebel ball out of him that time. Longarm had been hit in his own day, so he knew what everyone meant. There was something about having a painfully hard strangeness throbbing like a bitty extra heart under a man's hide to throw him off his feed and worry him all out of proportion to the actual discomfort. When one of the county men said Jarlsborg had taken one round in his upper left thigh Robinson said that was about as fine a place to get hit as any he could think of.

Longarm didn't ask why. He knew there was only one bone and one serious artery in a man's thigh and plenty of firm meat. So, unless a bullet hit the femoral bone or artery, such wounds tended to heal fast with no aftereffects, Lord willing, and there was no infection. Most old boys who didn't die right off of bullet wounds died a good spell later all pussed and feverish. That was one of the things a man thought about with a lead slug throbbing in him.

Once they'd all crowded into the modest lobby of the rambling two story 'dobe posada, Lieutenant Robinson told his second john to see about booking them quarters for the night.

Then Robinson ordered all the enlisted men but Corporal Finch to guard their shavetail, saddles, and such with their lives.

Longarm knew why they wanted Finch to tag along. Not too many had glimpsed even the outline of the Fool Killer through gun smoke and lived to describe him at all.

They found Swede Jarlsborg sitting up in the big brass bed of his cool corner room with a bandaged leg propped on a pillow atop the covers. The rest of him was clad in a baby-blue flannel nightgown. But he didn't look too sissy. Aside from all that wheat-straw stubble sprouting out of his big boney face, old Swede had a double action S&W .38 hanging handy on a bedpost and a pretty little Mex gal he introduced as his night nurse blushed fit to bust while she poured drinks all around, standing barefoot in her own lace-trimmed white nightgown.

Longarm had met Swede Jarlsborg before, albeit never to talk to all the much. The railroad dick was a few years older than Longarm and had an amusing way of talking, even when he was talking about getting shot in a mighty unexpected gunfight.

Longarm let others ask most of the questions as he had to smile some at the notes he was jotting down from time to time.

It wouldn't have been neighborly to ask if Americans talking Swedish sounded as comical to the average Swede. So he managed not to grin as Jarlsborg told his liltsome tale of dropping off a southbound combination for a quick looksee around and seeing a cuss who didn't belong there lurking betwixt the ramp chute of an empty cow pen and the waist-high end of that loading platform.

Unlike any other survivor to date, Swede Jarlsborg could say he'd brushed with El Matador de los Bobos in broad day at close range. But the more he described the cuss who'd answered a polite remark about trespassing on railroad property with a round of .45 in one thigh, the more some of the others stared at Longarm in a mighty thoughtsome way.

Swede Jarlsborg caught on, laughed incredulously, and quickly followed up on his terse description with, "Yumping Yesus, there was no resemblance at all! When I say the stranger I shot it out with was tall, dark, and wearing a mustache and telescoped Stetson I mean taller than me but not quite as tall as Longarm, there. His tweed suit was a darker tweed, almost coal black, and his features were different and much darker than those of our younger friend, here."

Robinson stared thoughtfully at Longarm as he blandly asked the wounded railroad dick, "How? If Deputy Long, here, was a shade more suntanned he could pass for a full-blooded Sioux."

Corporal Finch blurted, "Begging the lieutenant's pardon, but what if the rascal was, or is, a full blood? His first victim up to Camp Weld was a full-blooded Arapaho gal and that Miss Ramona he murdered at the Eagle in El Paso could have been part Indian as easy as she could have been part Mex. You know how some breeds fancy up their family trees, sir."

Robinson's pardon had been begged and to his credit he remembered it had been his own idea to have one survivor compare notes with another. So he didn't just tell Finch, flat out, to shut up. He said, "You've been thinking indeed. But we have the murderer of Arapaho Annie in custody down at Fort Bliss and who ever heard of a full-blooded Indian with the facial features of a white man?"

Longarm said, "I have. He called himself Woquini but we called him Roman Nose on account he looked like a Roman statue or matinee idol in feathers and paint. Some say his mama had been a captured French Canadian lady of refined appearance, but old Roman Nose was Quill Indian as they come."

He smiled wistfully at Corporal Finch as he added, "Unfortunate for the corporal's interesting notion, Roman Nose was killed up on the Platte in the Beecher Island Fight back in '68."

Finch insisted, "Neither he nor Arapaho Annie were the only fool Indians around Camp Weld and, like I said, I've been doing a lot of thinking about what happened to that Indian play-pretty whilst I was pulling Corporal of the Guard that fatal afternoon!"

Robinson decided he'd thought enough for an enlisted man and asked whether Jarlsborg's description of the shootist down in San Marcial matched that of the one who'd gunned Sergeant Plummer at the Eagle Hotel in El Paso.

When Finch agreed the one he'd shot it out with had been taller than himself, period, in a dark hallway filled with gun smoke, dang it, Longarm cut in soothingly to say, "Let's stick with things we know for certain, gents. We don't know, at this stage, exactly who did what to whom up to Camp Weld. If the army's holding the wrong man on that charge they owe him a handsome apology and meanwhile we can let him simmer at the back of the stove."

He was dying for a smoke but didn't see how he could light just one without offering all around in a mighty crowded room. Resisting such expensive temptation, he continued, "Actual fact numero uno. . . . A tall dark stranger gunned Plummer in the Eagle, mighty close to the scene of an even more disgusting crime."

Robinson nodded and said, "Plummer and the corporal, here, met him by chance in the hallway as he was coming from a wash-up he must needed, bad."

Longarm shrugged and said, "Mebbe. Sticking to facts, the same cuss or someone just as odd shot it out with me, shortly after, and when that didn't work he tried some more at twilight in the nearby railroad yards. He must have hopped the next train north for two good reasons. He couldn't be found anywheres near the El Paso yards and it wasn't long after my brush with him that he gunned Deputy Wilke in the gent's room of the Las Cruces Depot."

A Socorro County deputy brightened and said, "I follows your drift. The bastard . . . sorry, ma'am, has been working his way north. That's how come he shot this gent, here, at the jerk water down the line in San Marcial. The boys never found him in or about San Marcial because, by then he'd moved on north to . . . where? *Here?*"

"It's possible," said Longarm with a shrug, adding, "Figuring the possibles a homicidal maniac might find possible sure gets tedious."

Swede Jarlsborg frowned up at him to say, "Maybe that's yust an act. What if thinking he's crazy is yust what he wants us to think?"

Longarm shook his head and said, "Oh, he's nutty as a hazel bush in autumn, whether he thinks he's following some master plan or not. Sensible crook is a contradiction in terms, but those crooks with a lick of common sense commit such crimes as they planned in the first place and then they light out fast and far."

One of the Socorro County boys, being a New Mexico lawman, felt obliged to ask, "What about Billy the Kid, over to Lincoln County?"

Longarm replied without hesitation, "He ain't got a lick of common sense. Most everyone else mixed up in the Lincoln County War has been killed or run clean out of the county by now. So I expect to hear most any time how the Kid got killed or captured because he was just too dumb or lazy to cross a county line and change his name some more."

Swede Jarlsborg agreed it seemed a caution how El Matador de los Bobos haunted the Denver & Rio Grande right-of-way. Robinson almost put his foot in it but recalled just in time that the Eagle Hotel in El Paso was close to the depot and patronized by many a patron of the D&RG.

126

Corporal Finch chimed in with, "Camp Weld, too! I mean, it ain't what you'd call a railroad stop, of course, but we do have us a rail siding out there and there's all them empty barracks all the summer soldiers of the Colorado guard regiments built that time."

Lieutenant Robinson, being off another post, perked up at that and began to question Finch about another case entire. But before Longarm could say so they were joined by Second Lieutenant Chalmers, who said he'd booked them quarters but asked if by any chance their three enlisted men had come up here.

When Robinson asked what the shavetail was talking about, young Chalmers said, "I put Sergeant Hutchins and his men down the hall where people of quality usually quarter their servants, just passing through. As I was inspecting more suitable quarters for the lieutenant and myself in another wing of the posada I noticed the bed linens needed changing. I mean, they *really* needed changing. So after I'd seen to that I returned to where I'd left our enlisted men to see what *their* bedding was like."

Robinson said, "Very commendable and please get to the point."

So Chalmers said, "My point is that nobody was there. Since I had certainly never given them permission to leave I assumed they had to be eating, drinking, or whatever in some other part of this posada. But they seem to be nowhere downstairs, so . . ."

"El Paseo," Longarm cut in. When he saw the greenhorns didn't follow his drift he added, "They headed over to the plaza in hopes of making friends with the local Mex populace."

Robinson grimaced, then decided, "Well, they didn't disobey any direct orders and I suppose there's no harm done if the men enjoy a little off duty recreation."

Longarm shot an inquiring glance at the senior local deputy,

127

who shook his head and said, "If you're asking me if I'm volunteering, the answer is no. Anglo gents in this town know they're on their own if they're stupid enough to horn into a Mex social gathering without no invite!"

Longarm sighed and said, "They ain't exactly stupid. They just didn't know the rules of El Paseo in a tiny inbred town. So I reckon I'd best see if I can catch up with 'em before someone gets killed."

Chapter 14

Longarm figured anyone already pissed off about three soldados azules horning into a sort of private paseo would be at least twice as pissed off about six. So he insisted the two officers and the only remaining enlisted man, Corporal Finch, stay put inside the posada and let him see what he could do on his own.

It took some argument. The local civilian lawmen were as sure he'd never get those boys out of there alive without both a lot of luck and considerable help. But when he asked if any felt up to helping him out with their own wayward youths they all seemed to feel more married than lucky.

Longarm figured it was just as well, lighting up alone without breaking stride on the darker side of the way back to the nearby and mighty noisy plaza. He'd slipped in and out of semiprivate Mex gatherings before and knew half the battle was leaving their womenfolk alone and striking up a friendly conversation with more sensible Mexican males before the real assholes noticed you were there.

But even as he swung a corner to spy the full festive glow of paper lanterns ahead he sensed it was a mite late for a pussyfoot approach to the problem.

The problem was that none of those guitars he'd been listening to were still strumming and there was a mighty ominous silence in the crowded plaza, ahead, save for one hoarse Anglo voice bawling out to the tune of "Lincoln and Liberty too," off key . . .

"Oh, the gals in this town are so snooty,
   They fuck with their nose in the air,
      So whenever a man wants a blow job,
         He has to stand up on a chair!"

Longarm had just muttered, "Oh, Jesus!" and commenced to stride faster when he heard running boot heels behind him and spun to get his back to a door niche with a field of fire either way back and forth along the street, as need be.

But it was young Corporal Finch, a mite out of breath from his dash from the posada as he slid to a stop by Longarm and confided, "I thought I'd better warn you, seeing we're both Colorado riders. Them Fort Bliss officers must not have wanted to wash their own dirty linen in front of others, back yonder, but it seems Sergeant Hutchins can get really mean when he's been drinking."

Longarm nodded soberly and said, "*Loco en la cabeza*, too, unless that's another total asshole singing dirty in front of *mujeres* of all ages. You'd best head back to the posada, old son. Army blues could make you a handy target in the general melee that's likely to start any time now."

But the young M.P. tagged along as Longarm broke into as sedate a full trot as he could manage. He resisted the impulse to speed up as they passed under the line of paper lanterns strung around the two-acre plaza paved with stomped down 'dobe clay. The proper manners of conducting El Paseo called for all the gussied-up she-males to stroll one way around the plaza,

130

the he-males to stroll the other, and nobody to cut across the middle. But when Longarm spotted the singing sergeant and two troopers by a pulque stand in a far corner, surrounded by far-from-admiring male Mexicans, he forgot his manners and just loped over, diagonal, with the corporal right behind him.

The burly Sergeant Hutchins had stopped singing and hauled out one of those wicked-looking sabers all four enlisted men packed on their gun belts. As he spotted Longarm and yet another soldier blue coming in he called out, "You boys are just in time to help us learn these greasers a little respect for their betters."

Longarm knew at least half the surrounding Mexicans savvied his American this far north of the border, as he called back, "You're wrong, Private Hutchins. It's my painful duty to arrest you in the name of the law for the crime of singing off key as well as dirty."

He wasn't sure it was going to work, as he tried bulling on the rest of the way without actually shoving any Mex enough to matter. It might not have, had not a wiser head in the crowd called softly, *"Pero no, hermanos!* I think I know this one and if I am right he is not only muy simpatico. He has many friends, tough friends, among the parte libre."

That seemed enough for most of the mostly young Mexicans. But more than one still grumbled and Sergeant Hutchins grumbled like hell as Longarm's words sunk in. He raised the blade in his beefy fist for emphasis as he blustered, "Who are you calling a private, you fucking feather merchant? Even if I *was* a private you'd have no authority to arrest a fucking M.P.!"

Longarm knew better than to let his voice take on a soothing tone as he suggested, "We can let your own officers decide whether to bust you or not. Meanwhile, we'd best move it out. Corporal Finch?"

"Sir?" replied the Camp Weld man as all three from Fort Bliss eyed him in mingled disdain and drunken confusion.

Longarm said, "I'll take the lead back because I can make myself understood in Spanish if I have to. I want you to bring up the rear and cover the rest of us. I want you two privates to flank Sergeant Hutchins and make sure he dosen't fall down, hear?"

Hutchins roared, "Fuck you! I ain't no more drunk than anyone else around here! I was only trying to liven things up, gawd dammit!"

Longarm smiled thinly and said, "Bueno. In that case you'll be able to keep either of them from falling down. Let's fall in and move it on out, men."

Every army man but Hutchins moved to obey, however uncertainly.

Longarm knew it was best to give a military command as if one had no doubt it would be carried out. So having told the four of them what he expected of them, Longarm turned on one heel to lead the way.

He found himself almost nose to nose with a vaquero almost as tall, twice as broad, and reeking of pulque and peppers. He knew it was best not to pussyfoot around a bully-boy who was deliberately blocking your way, either. So he quietly but firmly said, *"No hagas fregadas, amigo.* I know these solados azules were out of line, just now. With your permiso, I'll be taking them with me, now."

The big Mex asked what might happen if nobody gave permiso to any maricon gringo. So Longarm smiled, not unkindly, and replied, "That would mean you didn't want to be my amigo and I suppose I'd just have to go right through you. *Que pendejo eres, hombre.* Can't you see I'm trying to do this friendly?"

The bully-boy pouted, "You say I am pendejo? You dare?" Just as Longarm heard a yell and a gunshot right behind him!

He came back down to earth a full fathom off to one side, having spun in the air and drawn his .44-40 to cover all concerned by the time he'd landed in a gun-fighting crouch to face that way.

Sergeant Hutchins was on the ground, writhing like an earthworm caught on a walk by the sunrise as Corporal Finch stood over him with a still smoking Schofield, saying, "Compton, get that asshole's sidearm!"

As one of the shaken privates kicked a six-gun well clear of his wounded sergeant before dropping to one knee for it the other demanded, "That was just plain stupid, even for you, Sarge!"

Corporal Finch said, simply, "I knew he was drunk and they'd told me he was a mean drunk. But I never expected anyone in this man's army to throw down on another man's back in front of this many eyeball witnesses!"

Longarm lowered the muzzle of his .44-40 as he rose to his full height, saying, "Neither did I and I owe you, old son. Where might you have hit him? He seems a mite confused."

The private who'd picked up the wounded sergeant's gun opined, "He's in about the same shape as that railroad dick, now. They both been shot in the same hams with a .45. How come you always shoot 'em in the leg, Corporal?"

Finch replied, lightly enough, "Had to aim low, just now, lest I hit someone else in such close quarters. Disremember why I shot that railroad dick so low in San Marcial. That's likely because I was with you boys, in Las Cruces, at the time."

Longarm said, "Let's not worry about any other gunplay till we get this poor back-shooting bastard somewhere a tad safer. Can you walk at all, you back-shooting bastard?"

Hutchins sobbed, "Shit, no, I'm the one who was shot in the back and I'm dying down here in the dirt whilst the rest of you laugh at me!"

Longarm glanced casually but soberly around as he softly said, "I know he's got a big ass, boys. But you two will have to tote him whilst Finch and me control a crowd that may have scented a mite more blood than I'd hoped to see spilt here!"

He was afraid he'd stated the simple truth when he noticed the big chunky vaquero and some other young Mexicans edging back their way again, after their first mass crawfishing from the roar of the corporal's six-gun. Longarm kept his own sidearm aimed down at the dirt, but handy, as a somewhat older and wiser looking Mex quietly suggested, "It is said among my people that an Anglo lawman known to them as El Brazo Largo can move quick as any pulga, even though he is big as a mulo."

Longarm answered, grudgingly, "Well, I ain't sure I cotton to being compared to either a flea or a jackass but some of my Mex pals have described me as El Brazo Largo."

So the smarter Mex laughed at the bigger and younger one before saying, "I knew it was him before I saw how he could move, and you were really trying to start a game of *Tu Madre* with him, Gordo?"

The big kid said the war was over, now that one gringo had put a round in another gringo who sang dirty songs in front of little girls and elderly priests. Then he turned to Longarm to ask if they were square.

As soon as Longarm said they were they had all the help anyone could have asked for in getting the leg-shot Sergeant Hutchins all the way back to the posada on a stretcher improvised on the spot from the canvas awning of that same pulque stand.

The officers as well as everyone else in a small town had of course heard the dulcet echoes of the corporal's six-gun. So they were waiting out front, along with some town law and curious folk of every description, as Longarm led the little parade up the way to them.

He'd been right about the way most army officers might feel about a sergeant who couldn't hold his liquor better than poor old Hutchins. Lieutenant Robinson had the wounded man's

134

stripes off his sleeves before the civilian doc they fetched could finish cutting away his pants leg.

Robinson told Longarm they'd handcuff the rascal to a bedstead and hold him under guard until the next train bound for El Paso and hence Fort Bliss came through.

As they stood out in the hallway while the doc worked on Hutchins, Robinson confided, "I knew he had a mean streak. I didn't know he was an all-out killer. You don't think . . . ?"

"No, I don't," Longarm cut in, adding, "He was a fool who almost got himself killed, just now. That don't make him the Fool Killer I was sent down here to stop, cuss his damned alibis for so many *other* shootings!"

Chapter 15

By the time they could have gotten back to Swede Jarlsborg and his pretty night nurse it would have been rude to go banging on his door whether he was asleep in there or otherwise occupied. So Longarm booked quarters down another hallway for himself with the intent of pestering the railroad dick some more betwixt breakfast time and that mid-morning combination he'd be boarding with those infernal army men who seemed to need nursing indeed.

When he'd asked if they had quarters with adjoining baths they'd told him not to be such a sissy. They'd figured they were mighty up to date for New Mexico Territory because they had indoor plumbing, once, on every floor. They advised him to carry a candlestick from his room down the top floor corridor to where a guest could shower down or even shit if he was too refined to use the chamber pot provided under each and every bed.

Longarm didn't argue. He'd stayed in worse places for more money in his time and he was glad they didn't have a bellhop handy to tote his baggage upstairs. For tipping got tedious and it did feel dumb to pack his saddle and such all the way from the railroad and then pay some jasper to pack it a few more yards.

Groping his way to a door his hired key fit in the uncertain light upstairs, Longarm let his battered McClellan and possibles fall to the bare floorboards just inside the door and thumbnailed a waterproof Mex match alight to see what he'd gotten for his six bits.

It wasn't so bad. The room was bigger than your average jail cell and the Spanish-style oaken bedstead and chest of drawers were proportioned big enough for a man his size. So he lit the fat beeswax candle they'd left him on the windowsill near the head of the bed before the match burned down to his fingers.

Then he forked the loaded-up McClellan over the foot of the bed, with one stirrup folded back across the seat lest he stick a foot in it in his sleep. He drew his Winchester saddle gun out of its boot and propped it to stand on its butt plate betwixt the head of the bed and the stucco wall away from the window.

The window was shuttered against bats, stray rounds, and such by cedar jalousies Longarm left the way they were. All the cool night air a man might need could still sneak through the slats and he didn't need any moonlight to protect him from the boogy man.

He shucked his duds slow enough to hang things that he usually hung up on the railroad spikes someone had neatly mortared in line as they'd laid that course of 'dobe bricks. His stovepipe boots naturally got to stand tall beside the bed while his gun rig was hooked handy over a sturdy oak bedpost. He put his wallet with his badge and ID, along with his pocketwatch and the derringer at the other end of his watch-chain, between the mattress and the solid oak bedboard. Then he slid under the rough but clean cotton sheets, bare-ass, and blew out the candle to see about some well deserved shut-eye.

137

Naturally, he hadn't had his eyes shut all that long before he felt a call to nature. Too serious to put off until morning, if he was any judge of his own innards and the odd dreams a man with a mighty urge to squat-and-drop-it could come up with.

Cussing whatever he'd eaten along the way that seemed suddenly so anxious to get out, Longarm tossed the covers off and swung his bare feet to the floor as he privately debated the advantages and vice versa of using the chamber pot under the bed or traipsing all the way down the damned hall at this hour.

He decided it would hurt less to throw something on and totter a few yards than it might to smell digested chili-beans, tamale-paste, and such all through the night. And it wasn't as if a man had to dress all that formal for a shithouse run this close to midnight.

He hauled on his knit cotton underpants, slipped into his boots without socks and drew his .44-40 for company, leaving its belt and holster on the bedpost.

He left the fat candle behind as well, lest he have to explain his half-naked appearance to any other late-night crappers wandering the halls. He failed to meet any on his way to the indoor plumbing. But once he'd locked himself in with a low-down commode and tiny sink in a windowless chamber of horrible smells he was sorry he hadn't at least brought some damned matches.

In the end the place was so small he could find everything he needed to just by reaching out in the dark. He was glad he'd been ambitious enough to pass on that chamber pot once he'd relieved himself of some beans indeed. The handy sink and a sliver of soap he found in the dark made up for the infernal slick-paper magazine some pinchpenny had hung on a nail by the crapper.

Feeling a heap cleaner as well as more comfortable, Longarm and his .44-40 headed back the way they'd come, walking soft, lest they disturb other guests this late in the evening.

So whoever that was in his room at the moment didn't hear his silent approach, even with the door ajar and a foolish amount of match-light spilling an amber stripe across the hallway floor and halfway up the far wall.

Longarm paused a few feet from his suddenly mysterious doorway and considered his options. Barging on in was a good way to catch a bullet with one's teeth, if some sneak had struck that light to jack a man as dumb as your average deer.

On the other hand the light inside seemed to be moving about as if someone had hold of it. So it was just as likely the sneak was going through his possibles, with some light on the subject and, son of a bitch if he hadn't left his wallet, watch, and such in there like a greenhorn camping in bear country!

"Easy," he warned himself silently as he caught his own legs tensing to spring like they knew what they were doing. He assured himself that what went in would surely come out and that the edge at such times was with the one lying in wait on either side of a doorway.

As if to prove his point the faint light inside was shaken or blown out and, sure enough, the suddenly black slit of the partly open door widened just enough to let one mysterious blur slip halfway out into the hall.

Then the intruder, and Longarm, were going the other way, fast, as Longarm hung on with one arm and shoved the muzzle of his big six-gun, hard, into softer flesh than expected, growling, "Just relax and flow with the current lest I blow your guts out, you sneaky motherfucker!"

Then they'd hit the edge of the bed and were going over, with Longarm fighting to stay on top, as his captive giggled in an oddly girlish tone.

They'd come to rest atop his bedding, his bare chest against a half open kimono, before she could say, more convincingly, "If there was one thing I never could have done to my mother or even your own, that was it. I'm on your side, Custis Long."

He left the muzzle of his .44-40 right where it was, probing her belly button as her kimono fell all the way open under them, and told her, "That's easy enough to say, ma'am. But perfidity, thy name is woman and I've been perfiddled with by experts, no offense. So let's start with who you are and how come I just now caught you burglarizing this room in such a friendly fashion?"

She said, "You're hurting my tummy and I'm Erma Farnsworth of the Baker and Norris Agency, dammit. I wasn't burglarizing your room. I was trying to make sure you were who you said you were."

"What did you decide?" he asked, not easing up one inch as he ran the muzzle of his gun down a ways to make sure she packed no concealed weapons where some she-male suspects had been known to pack 'em.

She gasped, "Jesus! That gunmetal is cold and when I *do* hide a derringer between my thighs I do so quite a bit lower. They told me you were awfully fresh as well as slick. I still had to make sure. You don't just answer to the description of the notorious Longarm, you know. There's this mysterious killer they call El Matador de los Bobos and . . ."

"Swede Jarlsborg's seen us both and he says I ain't him," Longarm cut in, adding, "Does Swede know you're on his case as well, or do you just sneak up on everybody?"

She said, "It's a long story. Now that I've made sure of your laundry marks, would you please take that gun out of my privates and shut the door so we can continue this discussion in private?"

He shifted the gun to his left hand so he could keep it handy to her skull as he ran his now-free right hand up and down her almost completely naked body, saying, "Not till I know you way better. What was that about my *laundry marks,* ma'am?

Where did you learn to read Chinese and what might them Chinese squiggles on my shirttails and such signify, in plain American?"

She giggled and replied, "You're getting to know me indeed and if you don't stop this instant I don't know how either one of us will be able to stop, you fresh thing! As for your laundry marks, I didn't have to know what they meant, as long as I knew they'd been applied by that Chinese laundry near your furnished room on the unfashionable side of Cherry Creek. I just told you I worked out of Denver, didn't I?"

He said, "You sure did, and that private agency has been getting their money's worth out of you, Miss Erma. I've noticed, my ownself, how easy it is for a faker to pack another gent's badge and ID. But your average crook would never think to run the brand of any Chinese laundry. Such marks are meant to be out of sight and almost out of mind, albeit I've used 'em, my ownself, to identify a body or more."

She insisted, "Well?" as he ran his free hand up her other naked flank. Then she suddenly grabbed his wrist to slide it down the full length of her nicely formed naked belly as she sobbed, "Oh, the hell with the door at this hour with all the lights out anyway! I've been following you so long and it's been so long since my husband got killed up in Cheyenne and . . ."

"Hold on, ma'am," he cut in, even as his questing fingers told him that whatever her motives might be there was no doubting the sincere wetness of the gaping groin she was thrusting up off the bedding for his full inspection.

The question before the house was still how truthful a hot-and-horny total stranger might be about other matters. He only knew for certain she'd snuck in here in his absence armed with nothing more dangerous than matches and not wearing as much as a sock under her brocaded silk kimono. But he wasn't about to leave her on that bed within grabbing distance of a Winchester and loaded derringer as he got off it. So he suggested, "Let's both ease up and go back to that doorway to start all over, less rough."

She moaned, "It's too late. I can feel how manly you've started to feel, inside those silly cotton drawers, so take it out and put it in me, you fool!"

Longarm pulled it back from her soft, slowly grinding hips, as much as that hurt, to growl, "First things first and if you really ain't trying to get me caught with my pants down, literal, I'll try and make it up to you. But, meanwhile, I don't even screw old pals in a strange town behind a wide-open door. So let's lock the damn door and have a better look at you before we get any more relaxed."

She sighed and stopped resisting as he rose, gun still in his left hand, to haul her up after him by one wrist and lead the way back to the door. She started to say something. He hushed her and she was smart enough to stop breathing, too, as he had a good listen out in the hallway. Somewhere in the night a baby was crying or a cat was fucking. It was too far off to say for certain. So Longarm nodded and said, *"Bueno. Mi casa es su casa,"* as he softly shut the door and tucked the pistol under an arm to lock and bolt the same.

. She tugged back toward the bed, sobbing, "Hurry! It's been ever so long, and you're so good-looking, and you already know I'm just gushing for you, right?"

He let him lead him back to the bed, as most men would have, but felt obliged to demand, "How come? Just what are you trying to pull on me, now, Miss Erma? I'd be lying and you'd know I was lying if said I found this situation repulsive. But it's been my sad experience that she-male suspects I throw down on are more likely to be out to fool a lawman as they are to fornicate for simple fun."

She hauled him down beside her atop the bedding and pleaded for him to just get on with it. Since he found his cotton clad hips now wedged in the welcoming V of her naked thighs he could hardly see his way clear to get out of it. His fool pecker had not only gone stiff as an old corn cob but found its own way out the front of his fly. So he politely aimed the gun in one hand the other way and let her sort of inhale him, to the roots, with a soft wail of pure enjoyment.

He enjoyed it, too, but cautioned, "Let's keep it down to a roar," as he just had to shove the .44-40 under a pillow to free both hands so they wiggled him out of his underwear and deeper in her at the same time.

She sure knew how to wiggle. She'd told him she'd been married, and happily, from the way she enjoyed herself with a man some gals took more time getting used to. When she held his naked chest to her firmly heroic breasts and crooned how much she admired a man who stood tall in every way he felt obliged to tell her she had a swell old organ grinder, herself.

That was the simple truth, as the sweet screwing stranger he'd never recognize in broad day gripped his shaft just right with her smooth legs wrapped around his waist. He'd figured out by now, from the few signs of time's cruel teeth he'd detected with his lips as well as fingertips, that Erma had to be as old as him or even older, give or take a rougher than usual life. So that was doubtless why her pussy felt so swell. He'd found out with other mature matrons of Denver that screwing older women was a heap like shaking hands, with a firm friendly shake counting for more than the size of the fist that was gripping you back. A gal who really knew how to hang on to a man down yonder could feel just as tight and one hell of a lot more acrobatic than some pretty young thing pissing and moaning about how much respect she might rate in the morning.

He came in her fast, as most men would have, but felt inspired to keep going as she climaxed in turn, more than once by the time he was there again just right.

As they lay panting for breath in each other's arms Erma sobbed in wonder, "We came together that last time and it made me feel so lovely."

He said, "Well, lovely is as lovely does, little darling. I hope you have other bad habits. Because I mean to enjoy a smoke whilst I get my second wind so's I can enjoy you some more. So would you rather share or smoke your own?"

She hesitated, then she pleaded, in a sad little voice, "Please don't strike a match, Custis. I don't . . . want you to look at me."

He had to study some before he gravely told her, "Now we're back to just who might be trying to cow-squat whom, here. I mean, you're a great little lay and I'm sure you meant at least half those nice things you said while we were coming together, just now. But I did catch you creepy crawling in here after midnight and, no offense, you did wait till I ducked out before you ducked in, remember?"

She insisted, "I told you why. I had to make sure you were who you said you were before we compared notes."

He snuggled her closer and decided, "All right. Let's light up and compare away."

She said, "Please don't. Not after . . . what we just did. I know it was my idea, but now that we have I feel so . . . awkward."

He didn't want to hear any more of that old she-male complaint. So he said, "I reckon I can listen in the dark if it's really that upsetting to you, Miss Erma. Are we comparing notes on that Fool Killer you feared I might be until you studied my laundry marks?"

She said, "Yes. Swede Jarlsborg thinks there's some connection between El Matador de los Bobos and those rumors someone's planning to stop the Denver and Rio Grande any time now."

144

Longarm asked what she thought. Erma said, "I'm not sure. It's true all those otherwise pointless shootings have taken place on or within easy walking distance of the railroad right of way. But aside from gunning men for no sensible reason the monster's actually fornicated with dead women. So who's to say what, if anything, such a lunatic could have in mind?"

Longarm shrugged the bare shoulder she didn't have her head up against as he replied, "Well, I reckon a cuss who could bite a dead gal's nipple off or draw on me because I asked if a newsstand was open could rob a train or milk an elephant if his heart was set on it. What does Swede say about the lunacy angle?"

She said, "Swede Jarlsborg doesn't know I'm on the case. He works for a different agency. The railroad hired us to check on *him* after he started filing odd reports about criminal plans that failed to pan out."

"So what have you reported about old Swede?" Longarm asked.

She said, simply, "Nothing, so far. While it's true nobody else has picked up anything about train robberies from the usual sources there have been all those odd crimes all along the D and RG right of way. As for reporting a few petty transgressions of another private detective. . . . Well, you did hear me begging for much the same just now, didn't you?"

Longarm smiled in the dark and growled, "Yep, and I'd be another horny pot calling the kettle black if I was to report anyone for a harmless affair with someone alive and willing. But I still want to hear about old Swede and any serious screwing he's been up to."

She began to fondle his semierection as she said she'd noticed how interested he was in the subject. Then she said, "He's been a tad bolder, or more foolish about such matter than I thought wise. Nothing downright disloyal to the D and RG, since the railroad widow he visits a lot down in San Marcial

145

can't be said to be committing adultery with a fellow employee of her late husband but . . ."

"So *that*'s what old Swede was up to in such an otherwise dull jerk water," Longarm cut in with a chuckle, adding, "I'm way more interested in what the Fool Killer could have been up to in San Marcial. I failed to see anything worth the time and trouble of a serious outlaw in the time I was there."

Then he frowned thoughtfully and tried, "Hold on. You say this railroad widow Swede's been consoling lives *alone*, within walking distance of the D and RG?"

Erma snuggled closer and began to fondle his semierection as she replied, "Never you mind about other widows who need consoling. Could I get on top, this time?"

He felt no call to argue as, without even waiting for a proper invite, the lusty lady threw a long limb across him to spit herself on his renewed virility. He understood why as soon as she commenced to bounce. It was small wonder she'd been pleading with him to move faster all the time he'd been on top. For she had an enthusiastic shake as well as a firm grip down yonder.

By this time she'd shucked her kimono entire and wiggled in a mighty pleased way, all over, as he ran his palms all over her. She said his mustache tickled, and she seemed to like that, too, when he hauled her down closer to nibble both nipples. But then they'd both come some more and she lay dishrag limp atop him as he gasped for air and hankered for that infernal smoke.

He was tempted to just light up. But he knew she'd feel he'd tricked her and, truth to tell, he wasn't really sure he wanted to know exactly what she looked like. He was afraid he knew.

When she finally rolled off, groping about on the rumpled bed covers for something, he quietly said, "I moved my .44-40 out of our way during our last breather, Miss Erma."

146

She said, "Silly, I'm trying to find my kimono. It's been grand and I can't begin to thank you enough. But now that you've come in me above and beyond the call of duty I'd better get back to my own room while we're ahead."

He hauled her back down beside him, growling, "Are you trying to call me a sissy? It's still inky dark and graveyard quiet out, and if I ain't got it all the way up at the moment I soon will have, you sweet little thing."

So she kissed him and snuggled closer. He tried not to picture the face he was likely kissing back. It was kind of surprising how kissable even a downright ugly gal could feel in the dark if she really knew her kissing.

But despite his brag he did need a few more minutes of rest and so they kissed and talked, then kissed some more until it was way less important what anyone there might look like in broad day.

But by now they'd gotten past the first excitement into that comfortable grind of old pals screwing as much for the company as the climax up the trail a piece. So while he was shoving it to her dog-style with his feet on the floor and a good grip on both her hip bones he casually asked why she'd been in the Eagle Hotel that time, since Swede Jarlsborg hadn't even been in El Paso that night.

She grunted, "Ooh, that's too hard if you want to go that deep, darling. I don't know where that other railroad dick might have been between the time I lost him north of here and heard he was laid up in this posada with a gunshot wound. I was hoping you could fill *me* in some missing pieces of the puzzle, once I made sure you were really you, I mean."

He began to thrust faster but more gently as he firmly warned her, "We may have too many pieces to work with as it is. Speaking as one professional to another, honey lamb, I've noticed that a store-bought puzzle comes with exactly the right number of pieces in the box. So no matter how confused you may be, at first, it's a dead certainty every piece means something and you won't end up with any left over, or missing, when you put the final picture together."

She said she knew that, but that she didn't have nearly enough pieces to make any sensible pattern, so far.

He said neither Quill Indians nor sex maniacs had to follow a master plan more average folk might find sensible. Then they both felt like turning her over and finishing right. So they did.

The next time she said something about getting back to her own room before her reputation suffered irreparable harm he wasn't up to arguing. He was really dying for that smoke and didn't want to break the spell any more than she did.

He naturally rose with her for a lingering kiss by the doorway. It seemed the least he owed such a friendly old gal. When he asked if they'd be seeing one another at the breakfast table in the cold gray dawn he was just as glad she said she had wires to send and a northbound special to catch. So, feeling sort of shitty as well as relieved, he kissed her a last time as he opened the door and said, "Adios, Lady Greensleeves."

To which she demurely replied, "Good-bye, and thanks for helping a lady in distress, Sir Gawain."

So she'd followed his drift, the poor old well-read widow gal, and that really made him feel shitty. But what was done was done. So he locked the door after her, lit both a cheroot and that dumpy candle, and got out his notebook to jot down some of the cleaner parts of their long conversation.

But all the time he was jotting down disconnected items he might or might not make sense of, later, his mind kept straying sheepish to the musky odors of perfume and she-male lust still rising from the bed he was sitting on, and to that dumb remark he'd gone and made about Lady Greensleeves.

He knew that since she'd called him Sir Gawain she knew the sad tale from the King Arthur legends. Lady Greensleeves had been this pretty little thing who'd gotten herself on the wrong side of some witch woman and been cursed in a cruel and unusual way, the folk at King Arthur's Court not having any Bill Of Rights worth mention.

Longarm sighed and muttered, "We got to stop showing off to our ownselves with dry jokes culled from the Denver Public Library. For the poor old gal must have known just what you meant."

He consoled himself with the outside chance she hadn't. For the fairy tale story of Lady Greensleeves had ended happy when she met up with good old Sir Gawain. Before that she'd been doomed to look pretty by day and hideous at night or vice versa. When Sir Gawain wound up married to her, some damned way, she'd told him it was up to him whether he was stuck with a grand-looking wife to appear at court with and an old hag to sleep with, or whether he'd rather sleep with a real beauty in the dark and have to eat breakfast with an old hag. When he'd said it was up to her, his unselfish nature had lifted the curse. It was too bad, in real life, there was just no way they could ever make Erma Farnsworth as pretty as she felt in the dark.

Chapter 16

La Señora Farnsworth had checked out of the posada when Longarm got around to asking, after breakfast and some telegraphing of his own. He got a few more worthless details out of old Swede Jarlsborg, who'd felt up to joining Longarm and the two officers in the downstairs refectorio, with the help of a cane, as they all had flapjacks and sausage with sage honey.

The railroad dick said he was feeling way better with the slug dug out of his flesh wound. But he still aimed to head back up to Denver for some paid bed rest. The railroad was being a sport about him getting wounded in the line of duty. So it was true good old Erma hadn't reported his real reasons for dropping off every now and again in San Marcial.

Longarm had no messages for Swede to give his home office once he got back to Denver. When he asked in a desperately casual voice about a she-male railroad dick called Erma Farnsworth the wounded Jarlsborg replied, as casually, he'd never heard of her.

Longarm wondered whether that meant old Erma was a good private detective or an awful liar who'd been something else entire.

He knew nobody there could tell him. The army men were anxious to get the gunshot Sergeant Hutchins back to Fort Bliss, lest he die before they could court-martial him. The same local doc who'd dug a round out of Jarlsborg had done as much for Hutchins. But a gun could kill a man a week or more after it first shot him and more than two-thirds of the gunfighters who'd lost, so far, had died of infection, well after the fact, confusing the shit out of many a grand jury in the process.

By the time they'd ridden all the way south with the moaning and groaning prisoner, Longarm had about convinced the prissy but not really stupid Lieutenant Robinson they didn't really need his testimony at an infernal court-martial that might take place days or weeks from them letting their own surgeon fiddle with the poor fool's shot-up leg. Longarm's most convincing argument was that he valued his own time too much to testify at any sissy Special. If they wanted him to hang around Fort Bliss that long he figured to press his own federal charge of attempting to murder a government agent in the course of a federal investigation and let the hard time at Leavenworth and Dishonorable Discharge fall wherever they had a mind to.

It worked on the wounded bully's post commander as well, once they all got there. For as Longarm had expected, the army preferred to wash its own dirty linen and whilst company punishment was one thing, a dishonorable discharge reflected on the officers who might have hung three whole stripes on such an asshole.

That still left Longarm and the military police stuck for heaps of other answers. For, mean as he could get with a few drinks in him, Hutchins just wouldn't work for either rape-murder or most of those other shootings.

They had a swell Signal Corps telegraph setup at Fort Bliss. So lots of wires got sent all over creation between the time they had Sergeant Hutchins chained to a cot in the post dispensary and the firing of the sunset salute.

Longarm had a last one for the road with Robinson and Chalmers in the officer's canteen and told them he'd let 'em know the minute he found out anything in town. Then he went out front and forked the army bronc he'd borrowed off their remount officer, since the fort was close but not that close to downtown El Paso.

Near the south gate he was hailed by young Corporal Finch, on foot, who sounded upset. So Longarm dismounted to hear the kid out in the privacy of the big bay's shadow.

Finch explained he'd heard Longarm wouldn't be attending the court-martial of Sergeant Hutchins. When Longarm said he'd heard right and explained he had bigger fish to fry the young corporal almost sobbed, "I can't appear against him *alone,* dang it! I'm a Camp Weld man and everyone there will be Fort Bliss!"

Longarm nodded in an understanding way and soothed, "A heap of 'em may be just as pleased to see him busted to buck-ass and maybe do as much as six months bad time, old son. You told me before you shot him he had a bad rep as a garrison bully, and it ain't as if you'll be stuck here forever after you testify against him. We're sure to have this other shit wrapped up and they'll want both you and poor old Fernando Nash up Colorado way before Hutchins gets out of the stockade, see?"

Finch said he surely hoped so and asked where Longarm would be searching for that mysterious Fool Killer next.

It wouldn't have been right to tell tales about a certain blonde who looked as pretty with the lamps trimmed or burning bright. So he just said he had a few folk in town to talk to and swung himself back in the saddle to ride on before the worried kid could pester him any more about his own damned love life.

Night had fallen total by the time Longarm reined in behind the funeral establishment of Alice Fischel. As he dismounted to lead the bronc into the stable he told it, "I know I want to see Alice as much as I want to know whether she's found out who Ramona might have been, Browny. But where does it say a man can't combine duty with a little innocent fun?"

The bronc didn't argue, being a gelding to begin with. Longarm introduced it to the mule inside and saw they both had water and some love-grass hay handy before he told his army mount, "We'd best leave you saddled and bridled out here till I make certain of our welcome. I'll be back directly, whether I'm invited to stay a spell or not, hear?"

As he ducked out into Alice's dark backyard he saw lamplight spilling out across the grass from that basement window. Moving closer, he saw the undertaking gal had soaped the inside of the glass, doubtless because of those pesky neighborhood kids she'd told him about.

So how come, he wondered, was he down on one knee like this, trying to see what was going on in there, when all he really had to do was knock on the nearby cellar door and *ask*?

He found a corner of one pane she'd missed with her casual cake of soap. So he bent over to peek through it, as almost any natural man would have, awkward as it made him feel.

Both the young gals down there in the lamplit cellar were nice-looking. But the teenaged Mex gal Alice was working on lay dead as a turd in a milk bucket and naked as a jay while the blond and even prettier Alice did awful things to her with that undertaker's trocar.

Longarm winced and swallowed hard as he watched Alice pull the long curved metal tube out of the dead gal and squirt at least a quart of what looked like squashed chocolate cherries into a sort of big brass cuspidor on a knee-high stand. He was glad the window was shut as Alice calmly drove the trocar up the dead gal's ass some more and hauled back, hard, on the pump handle.

153

He didn't see the other dead gal, Ramona, anywhere down yonder. So, since she was the only cadaver he had any business staring at that way he straightened up and moved over to knock properly on the sloping cellar door.

It seemed to take a while. When Alice did open up, she was at her regular back door, leading out on her back porch. So that was where Longarm headed, calling out, "Sorry, Miss Alice. I figured since you were working down in your cellar . . ."

"*Miss* Alice, Custis?" She laughed, obviously glad to see him as she continued, "I've been trying to get in touch with you. Nobody at the Eagle Hotel could tell me where you were. Someone finally came forward to claim the remains of your so-called Ramona Taylor. He was her father, an Indian agent from the Cherokee strip. His name was O'Ryan, and he had no idea where she'd come up with Taylor. He said her mother had been another Ramona from the state of Veracruz and that was no doubt why we had so much trouble finding any kin of hers in Ciudad Juarez, Estado Chihuahua."

Longarm sighed and muttered something about perfidity. Then he asked if Alice had made sure of the dead gal's so-called dad, since menfolk had been known to fib as well.

Alice said both she and the El Paso coroner had made the poor soul prove he owned the cadaver he was taking back to the Indian Nation. So Longarm said that was good enough for him. But, as he'd hoped, Alice said, "Well, aren't you going to come in for some of my, ah, tuna pie? I'm afraid I have a rush job downstairs but I can get back to her once I've made you feel more at home."

He followed her inside willingly enough, but said he'd just et when she sat him down in her front parlour and proposed some sliced ham and cheese.

She said, "Oh, Custis, I always wash my hands before I step away from a subject for even a moment. The poor girl I've been working on downstairs didn't die of anything catching in any case. She was stabbed in the back by a malo she'd spurned."

Longarm almost remarked on the wound not showing, from in front. But he never, and Alice continued, "They have her killer locked up and he'll surely hang, the poor fool. His defense will be that she betrayed him with another man. I've already told the prosecuting attorney the girl-child was one of those rare cases where virginity at the time of death can be sworn and attested to, if it helps put her killer's neck in the noose!"

Longarm said, "That sure ought to do it, especially if his side tries to sell that unwritten-law bull to a Tex-Mex jury. You sure *do* feel for the stiffs you work on, don't you, honey?"

She prissed her lips and said, "Don't call them stiffs. I think of them as *human beings* who just happen to be dead. Death is not a big boogy boogy or even a dark angel to those of us who have to tidy up after it, Custis. Death is nothing but a nothing when you get right down to brass tacks. A person who's passed on can't do for his- or herself as perfectly natural body chemistry runs down, in ways the living find upsetting. So we have to help both the living and the dead with our own modest bag of tricks."

Longarm nodded and reached out for her as he said he admired a gal who treated everyone so thoughtful.

She let him kiss her. It felt swell. Then she pulled back and insisted, "Let's not start anything we can't finish, right. I'll fetch you some coffee and the makings from the kitchen and you can make sandwiches for both of us while I finish just one last vital chore downstairs."

He let her go. There was no way to tell her he knew she meant to pump the waxen teenager full of red soda pop without confessing to watching Alice sucking all her shit out, before.

Alice left the room. He knew she didn't mind him smoking. So he reached for a cheroot as he skimmed his hat across the room to hit a window seat good enough.

But he'd just thumbed a match head aflame when he heard Alice yelling something. She sounded farther off than her kitchen and as he shot out the match and rose to his feet there came a couple of loud thumps he could feel through the souls of his boots. So he got out his .44-40 and got moving, calling out to her but getting no reply as he charged out into the kitchen.

There was nobody there. He saw the door to the stairwell down to the basement was ajar. So he yanked it open and headed down it, even though it was pitch black, now, where Alice usually worked on the dead by bright lamplight.

He called, "Alice?" and heard something between a sigh and a moan, somewhere near the damned floor in the total darkness. So he fished out another Mex match with his free hand and thumbed a light.

He was jarred as he did so by the sight of that pretty young naked gal lying crosswise atop the zinc with her dead thighs spread wide, his way, and her long-haired head hanging out of sight off the other side. He didn't see Alice anywhere in the dim flickering light. Then somebody had busted a whole chair over him, knocking the six-gun from his suddenly numbed right fist and putting out his match with the same blow!

Then he was fighting for his life with what seemed a bare-ass total maniac who kept trying to knee him, cut him, or both, as the two of them thrashed at a forty-five degree angle on the stairs.

Somewhere Alice was sobbing, "Custis, he's got a knife!"

To which Longarm could only reply, "I know. I got hold both his damned wrists and I sure could use some help around here!"

So Alice struck another match and gasped, "Oh!" as she took in the confusing scene on her cellar steps. Longarm was more busy than surprised to find himself wrestling with the smaller, stark naked, and astoundingly strong young Corporal Finch, whose barlow knife glinted almost as wickedly as his maniacal eyes as he kept trying to pull that wrist free and get down to some serious slashing.

Longarm had no idea where his six-gun had wound up, but he yelled out for Alice to start looking for it. There was no way he could get at the derringer in his vest pocket without letting go the frothing mad dog who, dammit, had a knee digging into some floating ribs, now.

Then he saw good old Alice rising to the occasion on the far side of the obscenely posed cadaver. Alice was bleeding from one corner of her mouth and she was sure going to have a swell shiner in the morning. But she came around the end of her work table armed and dangerous, with her undertaker's trocar instead of the gun he'd had in mind.

Corporal Finch screamed like a stuck hog, but hung on, as Alice shoved that long wicked probe up his exposed rectum as far as she could get it to go, snarling, "Mess with one of *my* subjects, will you!"

Then she pulled hard on the pump handle and the maniac let go both Longarm and his own weapon to scream, "Who blew out the lights again?"

Then the mad necrophile lay in a naked ball on the floor between them as the battered but damned game blonde told him, her dripping trocar still in hand, "I heard something moving down here when I stepped into the kitchen, upstairs. I knew it couldn't be poor Rosie, there. So I struck a light and came down to see what it could be."

She pointed the sharp shiny tip of her trocar at the body on the floor to continue, "He was actually fucking her, right on the table, with her only half embalmed!"

Longarm said it sounded grotesque either way and asked Alice how she'd gotten off so lightly.

She said, "I naturally shook out my light as he tore himself away from his first victim. He hit me with something, but not his blade. Knowing the layout down here better, I was able to elude him by rolling about on the floor until you came down the stairs with yet another light, God bless you!"

Longarm got back to his own feet, located his six-gun in a far corner and headed over to it, saying, "A gent called Fernando Nash is sure to bless us both, now. They got him locked up for lighting out, in blind panic, from the scene of this loco rascal's crime up at Camp Weld, Colorado. He *told* us he'd been pulling corporal of the guard that day. Who else but the noncom who wanders the post making sure everyone else is where they're supposed to be would have a better crack at killing and raping any gal he found alone during duty hours? He just now showed us how he avoided blood on his uniform whilst enjoying the favors of dead ladies."

Alice glanced more closely at the dead Mexican girl, blanched, and said, "Oh, dear Lord and praise Him for allowing us to invent mortician's wax! The little monster was *biting* her, too!"

Longarm nodded soberly and said, "It's a shame he didn't wait a spell. You did say that embalming fluid is mighty poisonous to bite into, didn't you?"

Alice kicked the limp form at her feet.

Longarm soothed, "I'd best go fetch some local law, now. I mean to let the army know what happened here, first. So you ought to have time to tidy up both you and Miss Rosie a mite before I get back. I'd sure put something on that eye if I was you, honey."

She said, "I can get a leech from the neighborhood curado, later. What about this murderous little beast, here?"

Longarm shrugged and replied, "Let him lay till the army sends their own Graves Registration crew in for him. It ain't as if you or me owe him anything but a sigh of relief, right?"

Chapter 17

There was no way Longarm and Alice could get at one another in private that night, what with everyone from the Army to the kin of that twice-abused Mex virgin traipsing in and out to ask the same blamed questions and make the same remarks about lunatics who might have been raised too strict.

But they had close to a week of occasional sneaky interludes by the time both the War and Justice departments had agreed Longarm didn't seem to be up to anything more useful around Fort Bliss.

He never said adios to sobbing she-males if he could possibly get out of it. But that pesky Lieutenant Robinson caught up with him in the El Paso depot as he was stocking up on reading matter and tobacco before boarding his homeward-bound combination.

The officer never offered to help as Longarm toted his saddle and such out to the platform. He said, "There's still a lot about Corporal Finch I just don't understand."

Longarm set down his load with a shrug and replied, "That's all right. I don't think he understood *himself*, neither. That true love in Denver he said he had was all in his twisted head. He

159

made her up to keep from going into town with the boys to get laid. He *liked* to get laid. He went out of his poor sick head when he got a rare crack at his own notions of romance. But he was too shy, or maybe too twisted, to just step up to a known whore, like Arapaho Annie, and ask right out for what he wanted."

Robinson grimaced and said, "The Whore of Babylon would hardly let you bite her nipples off unless you slit her throat first. I agree with your written report as far as that killing up at Camp Weld goes. After he'd had his literally wicked way with that poor Indian laundress he simply washed up, put his uniform back on, and went on about his duties as that day's corporal of the guard, knowing someone else was sure to find her and holler for him while he was somewhere else on the post."

Longarm nodded and said, "That's about the size of it. Finch had no way of planning what came next, but Fernando Nash helped a heap by running off as far as Old Mexico like that. I'm sure I put down what Denver P.D. wired back about old Fernando's juvenile record as an older boy who liked to play doctor with the little kids along his alley. He was way more harmless than Corporal Finch and he knew he never could have treated any kid so cruel. But he knew the law knew what it knew and that'll learn a cuss who don't know the country to light out for Ciudad Juarez."

Robinson shifted his weight impatiently and insisted, "I said I understood and agreed with you on that corporal's mania. I don't have any trouble with your theory about him spotting you and that wayward daughter from the Cherokee strip, up ahead, as he and his sergeant were coming south aboard the same train."

Longarm was beginning to feel impatient as well. That had to be his northbound combination backing into the siding, now. He told the officer, "I doubt he was interested in me. All three

160

gals he went loco with shared the same long black hair and dusky complexion. It might take a head doctor a month of Sundays to learn just why if the poor twisted bastard was still in shape to explain shit. So suffice it to say he slipped downstairs to treat poor Ramona as mean as he'd treated Arapaho Annie."

"But that was on the second floor. Why did he have to shoot his own sergeant on the third floor, blaming it on some other maniac?"

Longarm scowled and replied, "I just told you he can't tell us everything that was going on inside his loco skull, Lieutenant. The easy answer is that Sergeant Plummer simply got to wondering where the corporal had gone, encountered him out in the hall, and asked some questions not even a lunatic wanted to answer. We pretty well established he was an *impulsive* little shit who could act as reasonable as the rest of us, most of the time, and then snap like a twig and turn into a human wolverine."

The train he meant to board had hissed to a halt. He wasn't sure how long it meant to wait. So he bent to pick up his load some more as he continued, "He couldn't have known that pretty young señorita was lying naked, dead, and helpless as he followed me into town that night. Lord knows what he'd started out in mind to say or do as soon as I gave him the chance. He forgot all about it when he got curious as me about a lamplit low-slung window. He had no call to cut the throat of a gal who'd already been stabbed to death, so Miss Alice Fischel got lucky when she caught him in the act with a corpse."

Robinson said, "I know. I know. But Corporal Finch had perfect alibis for better than half those *other* killings. Both he and the late Sergeant Plummer were on duty up at Camp Weld the night those other M.P.s were gunned in the Eagle tap room, here in El Paso."

Longarm nodded and said, "I noticed. He was with you and Lieutenant Chalmers while Deputy Wilke was getting killed in the shithouse up the line in Las Cruces. Then he was with *me* as well as the rest of you when we all heard about Swede Jarlsborg taking a round in the leg up to San Marcial."

Robinson was more slow than downright stupid. He sounded sure as he nodded, "Then you agree it's now clear we've been coping with two seperate lunatics all this time?"

Longarm shifted his heavy McClellan to a less awkward position against his hip as he calmly replied, "Ain't sure the Fool Killer's as loco as poor Finch was. I'll let you know when I catch up with him. Right now I got to catch this train, Lieutenant."

He turned away to do so. Robinson almost wailed, "Hold on! Where do you think you're going if our case has only been half solved?"

Longarm didn't reply before he'd mounted the platform steps of the second car from the rear. Then he turned to call down, "I'm off to solve the rest of it, of course. I ain't the first who's noticed all the shadowy shootings of the Fool Killer have taken place within walking distance of this railroad's right of way. The railroad and both detective agencies they'd hired are headquartered at the Denver end of the line and I've talked myself blue in the face to folk down at this end. So adios and, like I said, I'll let you know."

Then he ducked inside before the pesky first john could waste more breath on things so damned obvious.

The train was a fortunate special, made up of unexpected extra freight and four passenger coaches, as long as the engine had such a light freight load. Longarm had been lucky to find out about it when he'd come by the depot to double-check his regular time table. He could see at a glance how few others had heard about the extra northbound. For his car was almost empty.

162

There was naturally no club car to the rear or dining car up forward. But, looking on the bright side, a man felt free to let his old saddle ride beside him on the seat and he could likely buy cold sandwiches and warm soda pop at stops along the line. Meanwhile he had plenty of smokes, a couple of magazines, and they'd likely make Denver in time for a late warm supper at the home of a certain Capitol Hill matron with light brown hair and a heavy way of breathing, once you got her upstairs.

The train started up with a knuckle-crunch of its couplers as a late arrival boarded with a carpetbag and some heavy breathing of her own, making Longarm mighty sore he'd left no seat beside his own foolish ass. For she would have been just the beautiful way to enjoy an otherwise tedious day trip through a heap of dull and dusty chaparral.

She was a willowsome but not-too-skinny natural redhead in an expensively tailored tan travel duster and veiled straw boater. He could tell from the way she looked the other way as she passed his confoundedly crowded seat that she'd noticed him as well. But what the hell, there were so many empty seats up ahead she'd have had no proper excuse to sit down beside a strange gent in any case and, sure enough, there she sat with her own baggage on the seat beside her as if she enjoyed the notion of a long day trip with nobody to talk to.

They'd rolled north a dull half hour or more before the conductor came back their way, the lazy cuss, to punch the few tickets of a mere handful of passengers. But it could have been worse. Longarm knew this one, too, and unlike old Max on the run down, old Angus rode this line regular and he'd been with the D&RG since they'd laid the first tracks.

The pretty redhead a half dozen seats forward gave him another grand view of her cameo profile as she turned in her own seat to jaw with old Angus whilst he punched her ticket. Longarm figured she was around thirty. Or just right if a gal

163

had taken it easy with rich food, strong drink, or brutal lovers. As she turned away again Longarm told himself to think about another nicely matured gal with browner hair, who'd be not only a more certain lay but a mighty fine one, if ever this confounded combination got them there.

Angus MacSomething punched a homely cowhand's ticket and got on back to where Longarm and his saddle were hogging the last seat against the rear bulkhead. Old Angus didn't ask Longarm for a fool ticket. He said, "Och, I ken ye've heard," in his sort of comical brogue. Angus had once said he'd been born on one of them Scotch islands where nobody talked English until they'd started school, and Longarm had suspected their schoolmarm of being a mite confused as well. But he didn't enjoy it when folk twitted him for his own way of talking, natural as it had always sounded in West-by-God-Virginia. So he just asked the older man what he was supposed to have heard about.

The conductor glanced about, as if afraid that pretty redhead way ahead was scouting for Frank and Jesse, as he bent over to confide, "Silver certificates. Ay, close to a million dollars worth of them, being sent to the Denver mint for redemption by the auld Bank of Mexico. Did ye nay ken why we'd made up this special at the last moment, Laddy Buck?"

Longarm whistled softly and replied, "It makes sense, now that I study on it. These day coaches and most of the box cars ahead are just razzle-dazzle, right?"

When the gray-haired Scot confirmed his notion Longarm asked where the express car might be, since he hadn't noticed any. He had to chuckle fondly when Angus explained the considerable paper cash was riding just behind the locomotive tender in an innocent looking boxcar, chalked as a shipment of alligator pears from Old Mexico. The funny fruit was for sale in the Mex parts of Denver. But nobody else was likely to be interested in stealing any.

164

Longarm asked who might be guarding the shipment to the Denver mint. He nodded in approval as Angus named a trio of railroad dicks he'd worked with in the past.

That reminded him of Swede Jarlsborg and Angus said the wounded Scandinavian was on sick leave, up at the north end of the line and doubtless spending a heap of time in bed whether he was sleepy or not.

Longarm smiled thinly and said he'd seen the pretty night nurse old Swede had found somewhere along the line. When he added he'd found the Mex community of Socorro so friendly to outsiders the more informed railroader laughed and said, "Och, she was nay fra' Socorro if we're speaking o' the same bonnie Conchita."

Longarm decided that had been the name Swede had called the gal who'd served drinks all around at the posada in Socorro. So Angus explained, "Ay, I thought so. They rode wi' me to Denver a few days ago. Bonnie Conchita is fra' San Marcial, or she was, until the other day. Before she met Swede she was married to another railroad mon ca'd Lansbury."

Longarm blinked and demanded, "Hold on, are you trying to tell me that was the Widow Lansbury old Swede Jarlsborg was supposed to be sparking all this time in San Marcial?"

Angus said everyone who rode this line knew that. Longarm added it all up in his head, nodded, and said, "All right. It all fits together if you figure a gent met a maniac on his way to kiss his true love. She'd naturally hear about it and she'd naturally feel free to cling to his wounded side, the lucky rascal. Do you know another railroad dick called Erma Farnsworth, she-male, say fifty years old and built way younger, save for her poor face?"

Angus made a wry face and decided, "Och, who'd want to? I've nay heard the name before. But, wait, I do reca' a nicely built aulder woman wi' a face that could stop a clock riding

165

this line, both ways, more often than most whisky drummers, noo that ye mention it."

Longarm decided he'd best drop it. Old Erma hadn't really lied to him about Swede Jarlsborg and that railroad widow. She just hadn't been offered a drink in the wounded man's room that same night and she'd *said* none of the regular D&RG men were supposed to know she'd been hired to check up on 'em.

Old Angus moved on about his duties. A million years and about fifty miles on they'd made it to Las Cruces. Longarm was surprised but not upset when they slowed down but steamed right on through a usual stop without stopping. He savvied their plan, now. They were out to razzle-dazzle anyone who'd heard about that big cash shipment. They'd put it aboard what they'd called a special combination to confound anyone watching the usual express cars in their yards and now they were out to confound everyone more by running a rinky dink day-tripper as an express flier.

He hoped they'd at least told a few switchmen up the line ahead. It could smart to go off the rails at this speed in cactus country.

The country outside got too bleak for any train robber with a lick of sense and the least regard for horseflesh. Longarm blew smoke rings that neatly framed the back of that redhead's pretty head, he doubted she could tell, as they rode on and on and then some. He'd been counting on them stopping somewhere along the way for food and drink, damn their hurry.

They finally did, over an hour later. When Longarm looked out he saw they'd stopped to jerk water at San Marcial, Lord love 'em and so where was the candy butcher who usually came aboard at such stops?

He got up and strode back to the platform, where he found old Angus smoking a stogie that reminded one of old Billy Vail at the home office. As men got older they seemed to

166

crave ever stronger tobacco. Longarm reached for a cheroot in self-defense as he asked Angus what the chances of some local tamales, at least, might be.

Angus said, "Och, the Mex bairn wha usually pesters the passengers hae been taken by surprise, I hope. There's seldom a train, this time of the day, and we'll be on our way as soon as they hae a few more buckets of water up oot a' the Rio Grande, ye ken."

Longarm muttered, "Shit, I'm hungry," before he lit his smoke. It didn't really help when a man was really hungry. He moved to the edge of the platform away from the town and leaned out to glare up the curved line. He could see the diamond-stacked Baldwin 2-4-4 standing midway across the timber trestle spanning the muddy Rio Grande. Someone was doing something. But the movement was mostly on the far side. He was about to pull back when he noticed that diamond-stack was puffing serious smoke and the whole front end of the train seemed to be moving on. So how come this end was standing still?

He asked Angus, who swung out beside him, gasped in astonishment, and wailed, "Och, someone's uncoupled the engine and that first boxcar! The one wi' all the money in it!"

So Longarm was on the platform with his McClellan at his feet when the first dozen or so San Marcial townsmen showed up, waving guns. The one with a badge Longarm had talked to the last time said, "There's a dead man sprawled at the water's edge under the trestle and the front of this train seems headed on up the line, lickety split!"

Longarm said, "I noticed. Never heard shot-one, though, and I thought there were supposed to be three railroad dicks in that one boxcar."

The local lawman suggested they ask the sons of bitches all the picky details once they caught them. He added, "Frank

167

Ketchum has wired up the line and the boys at Socorro will stop that engine or make anyone driving it sure wish they had. Meanwhile we're fixing to posse up and ride out after the sons of bitches!"

Another local who doubtless knew the country volunteered, "I'd have other pals waiting with ponies at Mescal Wash and be on my way to the Sierra Obscura before anyone could expect a train to reach Socorro if *I* was robbing it!"

A local vaquero snorted, "Ay, pendejo, Las Obscuras are too far and too open for such business. Any ladrones who knew this country would surely make for the much higher and much closer Magdalenas!"

The one with the badge snapped, "We sure ain't going to catch 'em here in town. So what say we get cracking?"

Another Mex shouted, "Sí, sí vamanos, muchachos!" and fired his six-gun in the air. So Longarm offered no explanations when he failed to tag along.

As they all headed for the municipal corral Longarm called out to a couple of Mex kids too young to ride off with your average posse. When they came closer, poker-faced and moving a mite tense, he asked if either of them wanted to earn himself two bits. The older one, about nine, said he wanted more than two bits if El Señor wanted to use him as a mujer.

Longarm said, "I'd rather have you watch this saddle till I get back or tell the law where I went if you hear gunplay and I don't."

They brightened up at the thought of such easy money and asked where El Señor might be, if he never came back.

Longarm said, "That's worth another dime to me if either of you know where La Señora Lansbury lives."

One pointed south and said, "The gringo fucking puta you seek used to live in a cabaña amarillento on the other side of those cow pens. Pero you will not find her there, now."

168

The other boy said, "Sí, she got to big for us and moved up to Denver, *la cosita perdida*. Is nobody there, now."

Longarm bent over and drew his Winchester from its saddle boot as he soberly told them that was where he was headed, anyway. He didn't get sore when one of them sniggered and asked if El Señor was feeling *manajado* this afternoon. He suggested they jack off, themselves, if that was what they were so interested in. Then he levered a round in the chamber of his Winchester and headed out, not looking back. He knew his saddle and possibles would be safe with the mean little Mex kids. Traditions more binding on them than a papal bull dictated that it was just as shitty to steal anything you'd been paid to guard as it was sissy not to steal anything a less *simpatico* stranger had neglected to nail down.

He decided a trackside approach would be a tad less expected. Hoping nobody was expecting him at all, he worked between the cow pen rails and the railroad tracks to pussyfoot south through shin-high cheat grass and tumbleweed until sure enough, he saw a small frame shack, painted mustard yellow and standing a tad apart from the railroad toolsheds and such at the south end of the cow pens.

There was no smoke rising from the tin chimney poking through the flat tar-paper roof. The blinds were rolled down in the two tiny windows facing him. He figured the door would be facing away from the tracks to line up with that cinder path cutting over from the dirt street running south past the cow pens. By the same reasoning, there stood to be no windows at all facing the noise and swirling soot of passing trains, just to the west. So he eased across the tracks with a view to circling those last railroad sheds and approaching the Lansbury shack from its blind side.

It worked halfway. He had no trouble keeping the sun-bleached railroad sheds and a wood pile between himself and those two windows as he circled out across the tracks

169

and through more serious weeds. When he saw he'd been right about the back wall of Conchita's cabaña he grinned wolfishly at the tactical error, even as he was making one of his own.

He'd get to sweat about it many a night in the future because he'd just eased past that cluster of tumble-down railroad sheds, his eyes and Winchester trained on the blank mustard yellow wall ahead, when a familiar voice called out, "Custis! Behind you!"

So he dove headfirst over a waist-high clump of greasewood to land on his rifle stock and one shoulder and roll whilst an angry swarm of bullets buzzed through the dust he was raising in quest of his goosebumped hide!

He kept rolling till he'd figured where all that fire had to be coming from. Then he risked holding still on his gut long enough to fire back at the smoke filled doorway of that one toolshed until he heard someone wail like a kitten down a well. So he fired again and rolled some more until his Winchester was empty and it got dead silent, save for the ringing in his ears.

Setting his saddle gun aside in some cheat-grass Longarm got out his six-gun, keeping his head down as he cautiously called, "Erma?"

There came no answer. If she hadn't been hit after shouting that timely warning she'd lit out again, the shy old thing.

He tried raising his hat on the end of a handy greasewood branch. When nobody even commented on the battered Stetson he risked enough of his real head for better look at that one railroad shack.

A thin but still visible haze of gunsmoke lingered in the dark slit of the partly open doorway. One booted foot lay visible atop the sunlit sill. Better yet, it wasn't moving. Longarm called out, "Give a holler or at least wiggle that left foot if you'd like to surrender, Mister Fool Killer. For unless you offer some sign of less lethal intent I'll feel obliged to fire again, no offense."

There came no answer to that, either. So Longarm judged about where his own balls would be if that was his own left foot sticking out like so and pumped three pistol rounds through the already shot up door planks.

The exposed boot didn't wiggle any more than it was supposed to, attached to limp meat absorbing hot lead and splinters. So Longarm reloaded his six-gun, picked up his empty Winchester, and moved in for a look-see.

Leaning the saddle gun against the side of the shed but keeping his .44-40 handy, Longarm hunkered low enough to grasp that one booted limb by the ankle and haul everything out into broad day.

The Fool Killer, for it could be nobody else, sprawled dead at Longarm's feet in a rusty black suit, Mex dandy boots with three-inch heels and a mighty bloody ruffled shirt. His nordic features didn't look all that swarthy with his bared teeth and open blue eyes glaring back up at the New Mexico sun. The chest strap of a shoulder rig gave away the secret of that notorious fool killing draw. Aside from its actual speed, a shoulder holster offered an edge in surprise. An innocently smiling stranger could be reaching for ID in a breast pocket as easily as he might be reaching for a gun.

Longarm muttered, "Don't look so smug, you sneaky cuss. I'd have had you pegged right off if that other homicidal shit hadn't thrown me off with his own goings on."

Stepping across the cadaver, Longarm kicked the bullet scarred door of the toolshed all the way open. His would-be assassin's .45 lay near the sill on the blood-flecked dirt floor. The gray canvas money bags and a more compact leather gladstone lined up along the back wall were blood flecked as well. Longarm knew what was in the money bags. So he scooped up the gladstone with his free hand and stepped back

171

outside, calling, "Hey, Miss Erma? We got him and it's safe to come on in and see what we just wrought!"

There came no answer. The homely but horny and mighty helpful old gal seemed to be acting shy about bright light again. But meanwhile a good-sized crowd from the nearby town seemed to have heard all that gunplay. So Longarm holstered his six-gun and got out his federal badge as they came wading through the dusty weeds at him.

An older gent in the lead with his own undersheriff's badge on one suspender strap nodded at the less ornate but more imposing badge on Longarm's lapel to announce, "Most of my boys just rid north after them train robbers and. . . . Lord have mercy, ain't that Swede Jarlsborg, the railroad dick, you just found, here?"

Longarm hefted the dead man's gladstone as he modestly replied, "I didn't exactly find him. I shot him. I had to. He was fixing to shoot me. In the back."

Then he opened the gladstone for a quick looksee before he got to half the questions everyone seemed to be asking all at once.

He snapped the gladstone shut again and set it in the dust near the dead man's head, muttering, "There are times an old boy can use heaps of material evidence and this could be one of 'em. I'd like Socorro County to impound everything in and about this shack till I can send a heap of wires and let the powers that be sort out just who gets what."

The undersheriff looked pleased but puzzled as he replied, "You got the rank and, even if you didn't, you'd still be the only one with the slightest notion of what's been going on around here!"

Longarm nudged the gladstone with his booted toe and began by saying, "He was packing his black wig, fake mustache, some theater greasepaint and the .38 he displays on other occasions in here. I reckon he'd have had way less

172

trouble boarding that forward car down El Paso way as a known and trusted railroad dick. But anyone who'd seen him earlier in the yards would doubtless recall a dark and moody stranger, see?"

Neither the undersheriff nor his two young deputies seemed to. So Longarm reached for a smoke as he strung words more carefully in his mind. There were now at least a dozen she-male faces in the ever-growing crowd. None of 'em seemed to be good old Erma, but he still made a mental note not to call either Corporal Finch or Swede Jarlsborg shit eating dogs as he recounted his recent adventures.

He'd just lit his cheroot when old Angus MacSomething elbowed through the crowd to announce, "Och, that was poor Sambo Brown they threw off yon trestle and the section master oop by the county seat just wired he'd derailed my poor locomotive and aw and aw. The mad reevers had wired the dead-man's throttle open and . . . Och mo mala! They've slain Swede Jarlsborg as well?"

Longarm heaved a smoky sigh and said, "I was just getting to that, old son. So why don't you all hesh and let me commence with the beginning and stop for questions when I get us up to here and now."

Nobody argued. So Longarm took a drag on his smoke and began with, "Once upon a time there was a fairly slick railroad dick they called Swede Jarlsborg. His sprinkled name was Olof, but that wasn't what he was sore about. He knew his railroading. He'd foiled more than one train robbery in his time. Yet he'd never been promoted, likely because he talked so comical and spelled some words wrong whenever he had to hand in an officious report."

The undersheriff sighed and said, "I know the feeling. So you think he decided to go into business for himself?"

Longarm shook his head and replied, "I don't think. I know for a fact he decided to retire rich as well as a mite early. First

173

he started spreading rumors about someone planning a robbery somewhere along this line. That was to throw suspicion off the very few who'd be privy to the scattered secret shipments of serious cash. Nobody as slick as old Swede thought he was would want to rob more trains than he had to."

Longarm continued, "He knew it was going to be a hard row for one man to hoe, working alone. He knew he had to work alone because most of the really good train robbers he knew were sore at him and, on top of that, he knew how often we catch thieves who've had a falling out with one another, and he was inclined to fall out with folk, the moody cuss."

Angus started to say something about Swede's rep for sudden fits of temper. But Longarm hushed him with a warning frown and went on, "As an experienced railroad dick, Swede knew robbing the train is nothing next to getting away with your loot, afterward. So before he made a grab for the gold ring he wanted to scout all up and down the line for the best time and place a murderous cuss working alone could hit and run. He didn't want anyone recalling a railroad dick named Jarlsborg anywheres near the scene of his serious crimes of the future. So he scouted in disguise, during his time off. Knowing the railroad game better than most of us, he found it easy enough to scoot back and forth betwixt Denver and the Rio Grande hobo-style or just riding as a paying passenger, at night, with conductors he didn't know personal."

Angus said he'd have recognized the rascal no matter how funny he'd wanted to make his fool self look.

Longarm growled, "I just said that. He made a point of avoiding anyone and anywhere he was well-known as Swede Jarlsborg. It came to me as soon as we met, friendly, why that darker, more mysterious cuss might feel he had to gun any fool who asked him any questions. But this suspect had another suspect setting up good excuses for him, and vice versa."

The undersheriff cut in, "Hold on, are you saying this dead railroad dick was that Matador de los Bobos who murdered all them poor lawmen?"

Longarm blew smoke out both nostrils and replied, "Haven't you been paying attention? He felt he had to gun most anyone of any importance who demanded any answer to any question. He couldn't open his fool mouth without making his sort of border-breed act downright memorable as well as sort of amusing."

Old Angus was naturally the first to follow Longarm's drift. He laughed and declared, "Och mo mala! His thick Swedish accent was aw' he was trying to hide wi' aw that blood and slaughter!"

Longarm nodded soberly and said, "That's about the size of it. When I brushed with him in the dark out front of the El Paso depot I was confused by another killer to begin with and then I wasted a heap of time trying to fathom why anyone would gun a stranger just for asking whether a newsstand might be open late at night or not."

He flicked some tobacco ash politely to one side of the cadaver at their feet as he continued, "I came out ahead in our sudden shoot-out. He was still able to run with my bullet in his thigh. But he knew I'd be curious about most anyone who wasn't supposed to be there seeking medical attention in El Paso."

He took a thoughtful drag before saying, "He works better than that other killer as the one who pegged a back-shot at me, later, in the El Paso rail yards. Then he just hopped the northbound freight he'd likely been planning on taking out of Texas all the time. He dropped off at Las Cruces for two reasons. That .44-40 slug in his leg was commencing to fester. So he was trying to doctor it with clean running water in that gent's room at the Las Cruces Depot when Deputy Wilke barged in on him."

The undersheriff opined he'd doubtless ask questions at such times and places, adding, "I reckon I'd have a thoughtful hand on my own gun grips shortly after I noticed a stranger with his pants down and blood all over the place."

Longarm shrugged and said, "Swede was on the prod and wearing a shoulder rig. Wilke just strode in for the usual reasons and I doubt he got to ask anything before he walked smack into a bullet going the other way. After fading away in the night some more as his sinister alter ego, this sneaky cuss turned back into good old Swede Jarlsborg so he could turn up here in San Marcial, where he had a logical excuse to be when he reported he'd been shot by that mysterious Fool Killer, too!"

A junior deputy snickered and softly declared, "Everyone knew about him and that railroad widow in yonder yaller shack."

The undersheriff muttered something about Conchita Lansbury not living there no more. So Longarm hushed them both and warned them not to get ahead of his story, which was complexicated enough.

As if to prove this he continued, "Be it recorded Miss Conchita ought to be up in Denver right now and she'll doubtless be more surprised than I just was to learn what Swede was up to all this time. I don't have to tell you gents how he staged a fake gunfight with nobody at all, just up the tracks, so's he could seek medical attention for the slug I'd put in him without my asking embarrassing questions. You gents were there and, if it's any comfort, I feel even dumber because, by buying his whopper, I set things up for a rascal who'd been wracking his brains for just such a setup."

Pointing south, the way the train had just come, rather than the way some of it had wound up going, Longarm explained, "With such a swell excuse for his wound, and time off from his regular duties, he began by moving the railroad widow who

176

owned yonder cabaña all the way up to Denver, leaving said cabaña locked up, empty, and guess who had his own key?"

The undersheriff started to ask something dumb about the closer tool shed. Longarm growled, "I'm coming to that. First, wearing his greasepaint, black wig, and fake mustache, as well as that suit and high heels he's still got on, Swede slipped down to El Paso as his other self. But just before our combination was fixing to pull out with a secret shipment of silver certificates he cleaned off his more familiar face and joined his fellow railroad dicks in their isolated box car up forward."

Old Angus protested, "Och, they were nae to do such a thing wi'oot informing me, ye ken!"

Longarm soothed, "I'm sure they knew that. Meanwhile a man you all knew and had no reason to doubt offered welcome help and his extra gun at the last possible moment. Once we were all well on our way he'd have had little trouble getting the drop on any three such trusting souls. We'll find out within hours whether he forced them to jump off a speeding train most anywhere we were rounding an outside turn in the desert or whether he just gunned them down like dogs and rolled them off."

The undersheriff stared south in dawning horror to declare, "Oh, Lord, I fear I sent my posse the wrong way just now!"

Longarm nodded and said, "Swede was hoping you might. Once he'd shed them other railroad dicks he only had to toss the money bags off as the train slowed down, this side, not the other side, of that railroad trestle. Nobody was likely to notice dull gray canvas in gray-green trackside weeds near an abandoned cabaña and some padlocked toolsheds. So he just had to wait till the locomotive and first few cars stopped on that trestle, up at the other end of town. Then, as the crew was jerking water he got down, strode up to join them, and forced them to jump off the far side at gunpoint."

Angus almost sobbed, "Och, that accounts for poor Sambo's broken neck and the laird only kens the fate of poor Engineer Thayer!"

The undersheriff nodded and decided, "I see how the rest of it went, up on the trestle, leastways. After treating gents who'd trusted him so mean he only had to uncouple the front end, wire that throttle open, and simply stroll away as confusion reigned a spell. So how did you ever outfox such a slicker, Uncle Sam?"

Longarm repressed a shudder as he considered how close a call he'd just had with a slicker indeed. Then he said, "We've all just agreed on the opportunities that trestle-stop offers a slicker. I liked 'em even better as soon as I learned about that vacated but still locked up cabaña, yonder. It occurred to me a man with a key of his own to such a place, and a good excuse to be seen leaving it, later, with say some boxes and barrels . . ."

The old conductor glanced inside the toolshed to declare, "Och, that *would* be a load for one mon to travel far wi'!"

"I make her a couple of hundred pounds, all told, in fifty pound bags. He was naturally gathering them up, down this way, by the time my familiar form hove into his view, first. I was thinking too hard about that mustard yellow cabaña a furlong south to think how much closer to the tracks this toolshed might be. He got inside along with his loot, from this side, as I mosied in mighty dumb from the other. Trying to back-shoot me as I was closing in on a truly empty shack wasn't the smartest move he could have made, but as soon as you study on him some he was inclined to shoot first and work out the finer details later."

The undersheriff whistled and said, "They told us you was good. What do we do now?"

Longarm wondered whether a lady playing secret agent for the railroad would want him to give her the credit she deserved.

Since it was up to her, all he decided to say was, "I already told you. We post guards on all this evidence, maybe put this dead rascal on ice, and wait for further instructions. Meanwhile I mean to send them wires I mentioned and it might be nice to see whether I still own a saddle or not."

He picked up his Winchester and headed for the nearby center of the tiny town as most of the crowd seemed anxious to watch a dead killer as if he just might sit up and say something interesting.

To their credit, neither of those Mex kids had run off with the saddle he'd paid them to guard. As he approached they seemed to be guarding it from that pretty redhead he'd seen aboard the train. So as he drifted in to join them he called out, "They wasn't stealing anything I own, ma'am."

To which she replied with something mighty vague as she lit out, blushing like the schoolgirl she'd doubtless been, say ten or more years back. As he passed through the space she'd just stood he got a good whiff of the perfume she still had to be wearing. As he got out extra dimes for the muchachos one of them explained, "She was not accusing us of anything, señor. She wished for to know if we knew of a private sala she could hire for the night if they fail to clear those tracks to the north."

Longarm scooped up his saddle and lit out after the redhead. It wasn't easy. She was moving poco tiempo in that flouncing travel duster. But he had longer legs. So as he caught up and fell in step beside her he murmured, "I won't pester you in public if you don't want me to, but I owe you and I thank you for that timely warning back there, Lady Greensleeves."

She didn't answer for a few awkward paces. When she did it was to sigh and plead, "Can't we talk about this later, in private, ah, Sir Gawain?"

So he said they could, and so they did, and so this time the old fairy tale turned out even more magical than in any fool kid's book.

LONGARM

Explore the exciting Old West with one of the men who made it wild!